Flight Against Time

Modern Middle East
Literatures in Translation
Series

Flight Against Time

Emily Nasrallah

Translated from Arabic by
Issa J. Boullata

The Center for Middle Eastern Studies
University of Texas at Austin

Library of Congress Catalogue Card Number: 97-077534
ISBN: 0-292-75564-3

Printed in the United States of America

Cover photograph: Jasper Brinton, published in *Aramco World*,
Vol. 23, No. 4
Cover design: Stan Kearl
Book design: Diane Watts
Book editor: Annes McCann-Baker

Introduction

Lebanon has imported and exported people for centuries. Lebanon's narrow coastal plain, embraced by the rapidly rising Anti-Lebanon mountains, which cascade into the Baalbeck central valley, has created a concentrated variety of ecological niches. The differentiated niches have hosted minorities and dissidents of almost every religious, ethnic, and political stripe in the Middle East. As a result, Lebanon historically has been a haven for people escaping political, economic, social , religious, and ethnic upheaval in the neighboring regions. Its relatively open political atmosphere, laissez-faire market economy, and by regional standards highly educated and cultured society, with relatively more advanced standards of living, has invited long- and short-term immigration. In its current dimensions, approximately 135 miles by 50 miles (4,020 square miles), and for its current population, about 4 million, Lebanon boasts a higher concentration of diversity (18 legally recognized religious sects) than any of the near countries including Syria, Israel, Jordan, Iraq, and Turkey.

While a beacon to neighboring peoples, Lebanon has exported its own people for centuries as well. Lebanese ventured out for trade, political conquest or to escape domestic upheavals. Since the mid-nineteenth century, Lebanon has exported hundreds of thousands of its children. Called "mughatribeen"(meaning literally those who go to the West), Lebanese emigrants have remained a backbone of Lebanon's economy (they send millions of dollars in remittances), culture (they bring back ideas and materials from all over the world), and politics (they continue to vote and influence local and national events). Most Lebanese emigrated with the expectation of returning. Many, in fact, reversed migrations repeatedly. Those going to Africa often sent their children back for a Lebanese education and returned themselves permanently, either by will or by expulsion. For most emigrants, however, their journey abroad was definitively one-way.

The peasant uprisings and civil wars of the mid- to late-nineteenth century saw the departure of 25 percent of the population, largely Christian. The famines and impoverishment during and immediately after World War I led to tens of thousands of Lebanese seeking their welfare mostly in North and South America, although many also went to Africa and Australia. World War II was followed by another stream of immigrants, retracing the networks of relatives who had already established communities abroad. This wave had a higher representation of Muslims than earlier migrations. By the 1970s, it was common knowledge that more Lebanese lived outside of Lebanon than inside. By one report, there were as many Lebanese in Brazil as in Lebanon. The most recent large exodus of Lebanese was provoked by the Civil War that devastated the country from 1975 to 1990, taking a toll of over 150,000 lives and hundreds of thousands of maimed and injured. After the 1990 Taif agreement, which brought some peace to the warring factions of Lebanon, thousands of Lebanese have begun to return. For many, however, the ending of the war is too late. They and their children now belong to other lands.

The Civil War of 1975-1990 forms a backdrop to Emily Nasrallah's *Flight Against Time*, but the story Nasrallah tells is far older and more universal than the Lebanese Civil War of 1975-1990. Nasrallah eloquently captures the enduring anguish of parents whose children feel they must spread their wings in other lands, touched by the "contagion of emigration," never to return to the "nursery that embraced the seedlings for a while" (p. 48). Her narrator is 70-year-old Radwan, an uneducated, orphaned, Shi'a Muslim peasant who, through hard work and personal integrity, manages to marry an educated young woman and eventually inherit her family's land. Abu Nabeel (Radwan's term of address, which means the father of his eldest son, Nabeel) and his wife Um Nabeel are invited to visit their five children, all of whom have migrated to Prince Edward Island in Canada before the beginning of the Lebanese Civil War. Both Abu Nabeel and Um Nabeel have siblings who emigrated from Lebanon so many years earlier that they not only have lost contact with them, but no longer know what they look like. The visit takes place at the beginning of the war in 1975.

Through the eyes of Abu Nabeel, Nasrallah helps us view the tearing of personal and social fabric when parents are separated from children, spouse from spouse, brother and sister from siblings, and friends and neighbors are uprooted from their soil. The village crazy woman, Roseanne, knows the importance of being rooted in one's own piece of earth where "man lived within the circle of his little world in dignity — honored and protected" (p. 32). She sends a small bag of village soil with Abu Nabeel as her present to his children.

The journey of Abu and Um Nabeel to see their children in Canada is an existential journey, a journey of the soul into the deepest moment of meaning. For these village people, the life is lived through and for their children. Abu Nabeel not only sees his five children as one person (p. 97), but sees them as one with him. While Um Nabeel recognizes that the children, all married, now have lives of their own and she is a guest in their house, Abu Nabeel continues to try to direct their lives, since the very meaning of his own existence resides in theirs. That he cannot speak a common language with his own grandchild is beyond his comprehension. The old have lived their lives waiting for the young (p. 7), but they have been cut off, their hearts ripped out, the house empty (p. 10).

For Abu Nabeel's children, the solution is for the parents to relinquish their beloved village, their natal country, and come live with them. How can the young know what the soil means to the old? The old are planted in the soil and can be uprooted only at risk of death. And while the seedlings are nursed in the soil, they are transplanted young at apparently a less life-threatening moment. Yet all who are woven into the family suffer from the tearing of the familial fabric. Semi-freed from the warp and woof of family ties, Abu Nabeel's children are neither unhappy nor content. Enduring the wounds of separation, they reconstitute themselves in their new homes: a reconstruction that is less than satisfying for the old.

In a tale of mythic proportions, Nasrallah captures the searing love of parents for children and children for their parents, despite two decades of separation, and sister for brother, despite half a century of separation. She portrays the yearning for loved ones from whom one will forever be separated, not by death, but by distance. In a world of global migrations, no one can be untouched by stories of separation, yearning for loved ones far away, and nostalgia for a time when parents, children, family, friends and neighbors lived in a small world of integrity and dignity.

Suad Joseph
University of California at Davis
1997

To the memory of my parents

1

The "problem" began at the Canadian Consulate in Beirut. It was the second day of September, 1975.

The appointment was written down on a piece of paper that he held tightly in his hand. He kept feeling it every so often lest it should fly away, slip from his hand or melt in the burning heat of his palm.

The appointment was written down. He had repeated it to himself so many times that he now knew it by heart: "Eleven o'clock before noon." It was now five minutes to eleven. Radwan found himself before an amazing box which would do his bidding at the press of a button, *at your service, on the double.* This was no legend or myth. This was reality, here in modern Beirut.

He tried to remember the year he had last been to the constantly changing city. His memory failed him but he recalled very well that this amazing invention was not known at that time. Press a button and move from the earth to somewhere near the sky? What a wonder!

This was not a button — this was the ring of a genie. He did not dare touch it but left the task to Simaan Al-Abras, his companion.

Like him, Simaan had come because he had been given an appointment. He too had papers from the Consulate.

"God help us!" Radwan exclaimed as he stepped through the opening. The door closed and the box shot upwards like a rocket. "God help us!"

His heart beat in a strange way. He whispered, "What is the matter with you, man? Not even beasts of the forest can frighten you. Why are you afraid of this interview?" He laughed at himself and answered. "Your fear of the interview is a future fear. The cause of your present fear is this rocket."

True. His knees were shaking. It was a new experience. "Lord, deliver us from tribulations!" he said and turned to Simaan. He saw him standing calmly like a statue.

2

From where did Simaan summon that courage, he wondered. He knew him to be a coward who trembled at the flutter of a partridge. He remembered his cowardice during a nocturnal hunting trip. The boy had practically passed out from fear. Since that day, he had begun telling stories about Simaan and making fun of him in anecdotes which he told among circles of friends as they sat on the stone benches of the village.

And yet, here was Simaan in front of him: a young man, the same age as his youngest son, standing in this amazing box and not batting an eye, appearing as if he were right at home.

There were people who showed courage in desolate forests, Radwan thought, on dark nights, in storms. And there were others who did not experience the life of the wilderness but were tamed by the city until they became its suckling children. Simaan was of the latter group. Radwan felt satisfied with that equation — and with the unexpected opening of the door. Simaan interrupted his train of thought.

"Uncle Radwan, we get off here." Radwan followed him with a jump as if the cursed box had given him a farewell thump on the back.

Is this how you bid your guests farewell, O people of Beirut? His question remained unspoken within his heart.

Simaan went forward and stood in a long line. He asked Radwan to stand in front of him.

"We will wait our turn, Uncle Radwan."

Radwan's lips parted to ask a question but he changed his mind. Simaan understands these matters much better than I do, he thought.

He passed the time by watching the strange faces around him and the backs of the heads lined up in front of him. Soon afterward he heard the sweet sound of someone calling his own name.

"Radwan Abu Yusef!"

He answered in a loud voice, "Present, here. Yes, I am ready."

His response was spontaneous. He did not wait for Simaan to signal to him but stepped out of the line and hurried toward the corner. The person who had called was sitting behind a glass wall that had a little opening so he could talk with people on the other side.

3

"Are you Radwan Abu Yusef?"

He answered enthusiastically, "Yes, I am Abu Nabeel."

The voice asked in a rebuking tone, "Abu Yusef or Abu Nabeel?"

"Both. Abu Yusef is my family name and Abu Nabeel, my familiar name. My eldest son is called Nabeel, may God protect your children and mine."

He said nothing more and fell silent, for he did not meet with any encouragement from the official. The man had not even raised his head from the paper in front of him.

"Are you ready to meet the Consul?" the man asked abruptly.

Radwan puffed up his chest."

"By all means. I am ready and prepared."

"Enter through this door."

"Thank you. May God give you long life and increase your blessing."

On his way to the door, he remembered to look for Simaan. He saw him still standing in his place and received an encouraging smile for him to go on.

"Alone?" Radwan asked in bewilderment.

"Yes," Simaan answered. "The secretary will help you."

"As God wills. We trust in God."

He said it aloud as if the people around him had vanished and he was left alone, facing the "problem" and the closed door.

4

Suddenly the door opened wide. Radwan was terrified.

The two halves had opened from inside as if by a magic hand, one to the right and one to the left. A fair-haired young man looked out and eyed him intently, then signaled for him to enter.

Would this be the Consul, Radwan wondered.

He regretted not asking about the color and shape of the Consul. But the hand beckoned insistently and the young man muttered a few words which entered Radwan's ears but did not make any sense.

The man motioned to him again. Radwan moved forward, in spite of the confusion he felt. He moved with firm steps, but once inside his heart beat rapidly. At the same time a voice within was quick to chide him:

"Shame on you, man. Look at him. He is just like you, a mere human being. He is neither a lion nor a hyena. As for you, even wild beasts don't frighten you, and...."

The young man left him no opportunity to continue his musings. He started to wave a metal instrument around Radwan's head, then ran it down his sides and under his armpits before passing it between his legs.

What was the man doing?

He felt tears coming and wished Simaan was next to him. If he was here, he would explain what this man was doing with this silver stick, whether he was the Consul himself, whether he was sane or insane, whether this was a greeting in the Canadian way, and what sort of country this could be that Radwan was traveling to.

The man turned his back to him, motioning for him to follow. Radwan walked after him obediently. The game was not over yet — there would be more surprises. God help us.

He had hardly finished his thought when an elegant and graceful young woman appeared at the door, her face as bright as the sun. He smiled in admiration and stretched out his hand to her. The young woman shook his hand and spoke to him in Arabic.

"You're an Arab, ma'am?" he asked. He had wanted to say, "Sister of my soul, my rescuer, my blessing from heaven: save me!"

She answered briefly, "I am the Consul's secretary. Do you speak English or French?"

"Your humble servant can barely cope with Arabic, let alone...."

She suppressed a smile. "That's all right. No problem. I will act as interpreter between you and the Consul. Please, come with me."

"Thank you in advance, daughter of goodness."

The echo of the last word fell on the ears of the unknown man behind the desk. He did not stand up when Radwan approached, nor did he stretch out his hand, but merely gestured for him to sit down.

Radwan was not surprised at this indifference.

As he did not know their language, they had to speak to him with signs. But this guardian angel was next to him. She must have come down from heaven. An angel, indeed.

5

"The Consul asks you, Mr. Radwan, why are you going to Charlottetown?"

"Aha! The Consul, then, was interested in him. He must have misunderstood when the Consul did not rise up from his chair and welcome him warmly.

"Tell him, in order to visit the young ones."

"And who are the young ones, Mr. Radwan?"

"My children: Nabeel, the eldest son, may God keep him and other people's children; Hassan, the owner of the biggest restaurant in Charl'ton; Jameel, who has a hairdresser's salon; Lamya, she is married to the son of the *mukhtar* or headman from our village; and Nawal, she teaches at the university."

"The Consul says, may God keep them. How many years have they been in Canada?"

"Tell him, my daughter, they have been there for twenty years. Nabeel left in the harvest season when he was seventeen. He had several jobs there and when God helped him prosper, he began taking his brothers and sisters, one by one... Tell him, my daughter, that they used to help me here in difficult times. After they went off to school, the land could no longer support us."

"The Consul asks you, how long are you going to stay in Canada?"

"May God bless the Consul's home... The children said six months. It's just a visit that my wife, Um Nabeel, and I will pay to get to know our grandchildren. Do you think the grandchildren speak Arabic?"

"The Consul would not know that, Mr. Radwan. But he asks you, how much money are you taking?"

"From God's abundance, and the Consul's, there is enough money. The young ones have been generous."

"Mr. Radwan, the Consul is asking about the figure, the quantity."

"We have one thousand dollars. When we arrive, the young ones will be responsible for our expenses."

"Very good. The interview is over. Here is your passport with the visa, and this is your wife's. The Consul has stamped them and he wishes you a happy trip."

"May God bring you and all people happiness."

6

Radwan took the two passports and felt that all the burdens of the universe had been lifted from his shoulders.

He leapt up with the agility of a playful child. He bade the Consul farewell by shaking his hand, unconcerned about the surprised look on the man's face. He shook hands warmly with the secretary and wished her all the goodness of the earth. Then he hurried out.

7

Where was Simaan?

When he did not see him in line, he almost shouted in despair. Did Simaan leave him and go? No, that was impossible. What would he do if this did happen? Where would he go, he who did not know the city? He had put all his trust in Simaan.

Just then, Simaan came out of an adjoining room carrying papers. Radwan's face gleamed as he announced in a loud voice the good news.

"We've got the 'bazzbort' and the Consul's interview is over. A great man, may God keep him and his family."

Simaan was not yet finished, so he led Radwan to a nearby seat and asked him to wait until they could both leave together.

8

It is true that the first action was at the Canadian Consulate in Beirut. But every beginning has another beginning. The first one came with a registered letter addressed to Radwan Abu Yusef. It was from his eldest son, Nabeel, which said:

Dear Parents,

After greeting you and kissing your hands, I am writing to inform you that I met with my brothers and sisters, and we agreed that you should visit us in Canada for at least six months, so we may see you and you may get acquainted with your grandchildren. We corresponded with the Canadian Consul in Beirut regarding this matter and sent him all the required documents. All that is left for you to do is to go to the

Consulate when you are summoned to obtain the visa and then decide when you will travel.

Enclosed you will find a check for one thousand dollars and your tickets for the trip. Please let us know the date when you will leave and we will meet you when you arrive.

Remain in peace and safety.

Your loving son,
Nabeel

9

The letter struck Radwan and his wife like a thunderbolt. The idea of traveling had never crossed their minds.

Travel was for the young people. As for the middle-aged and the old, they stayed behind. They lived their lives waiting: waiting for letters and the return of the loved ones.   The old hardly ever traveled.

At sunset, they would lean into the edge of the horizon and watch the sun move along the path drawn millions of years ago. It moved in its daily journey, from East to West, from East to West. Radwan and his wife were traveling to the West, to the *Gharb*.

That is why Oriental Arabs called emigration *ightirab* (going West, becoming alien) and *ghurba* (being in the West, being in alien lands). For outside their homeland, they were *ghuraba'* (aliens).

Here, they were in their own homeland, the homeland of their fathers and forefathers, and of their children and future grandchildren.

"But where are the grandchildren? Where are the children?" the man asked himself, not believing his present reality, as though the children had just left him that very moment and not twenty years earlier. His inner self answered, "They left. They went away. You bade them farewell at the edge of the village. You were afraid and did not go down to Beirut to see them off. Um Nabeel accompanied them one by one to the sea, the last boundary, while you remained here, implanted like a post in solid ground. That day, you were a coward, man."

Radwan bent his head as if the years had gathered their troops to invade him, to conduct a vengeful surprise attack on him, unarmed as he was and bereft even of words.

He pushed a chair to the edge of the porch, then sat down with his head propped up on his hands. He let his eyes roam about as he looked at the surrounding scenery.

Here was the village forest and there, scattered over the hill, were the homes of Al-Khalwat, the quiet and peaceful village which was the neighbor of Jurat Al-Sindyan. And over there, in the bosom of the hillside ascending toward Mount Hermon, were ancient monuments that went back hundreds of years and were proof that this part of the world was planted in the heart of history. Yonder was Tallat Al-Sheykh covered with fresh pine trees. And towering behind it was the chief of all mountains, Mount Hermon, proudly looking around as if to challenge everything that surrounded it.

"How can one who adorns his eyes with the light pouring from your peaks ever forget you?"

He turned to one side and saw the remains of the neighbor's roof tiles and a wall about to collapse. That was the wall of his neighbor, Um Said.

"How often have I warned her! How often have I said to her: 'Um Said, the wall exposes the neighborhood children to danger. Its stones are unsteady, a breeze would send them flying off.'"

But Um Said would turn a deaf ear and walk away.

Then one day she broke her silence.

"How can you ask me to pull down the wall? Don't you see that it props up the vine?"

In anger he laughed, and silently heaped curses on her. "That grey-haired, ill-omened witch! To her the vine is worth more than the children!"

10

And now, here he was, about to go on a trip. He would leave behind him the roof tiles, which now resembled a honeycomb because of an air raid attack by the Israeli air force. It was a direct hit on the house that did not spare even the trees of the garden. The family was saved by God's grace alone.

God, may He be praised and exalted, did not want him to depart this life so early and saved him from a piece of shrapnel that grazed his forehead. Now he was going on a trip and leaving this wall that was about to collapse. After much deep thought, he arrived at a solution: he would not leave until the wall was pulled down, even if it was against the will of Um Said. He would get the young men of the neighborhood to help him. He would urge them to attack the wall with their sledge hammers and pickaxes on a moonless night, and Um Said would have to accept a *fait accompli* and the opinion of the majority.

Before he had finished making this resolution, he heard Um Nabeel calling, "Your coffee is ready."

"Bring it over," he said. "And come here, let's drink it together."

In an instant she was next to him carrying the Aleppo brass tray that held the coffee pot and cups, the air rich with the aroma of cardamom.

11

"I see you are lost in thought, husband. What is the matter?" His wife was surprised at her own boldness, startled by her daring question.

Normally, she was the one who waited for his questions and then answered them, for his requests and then complied with them, for his motions and then accompanied them. To dare break the circle with a question...that was a rare event, especially when he was lost in thought as he seemed to be now.

He raised his eyes and looked intently at her as though seeing her for the first time. In her face he saw contentment and peace, in her eyes, goodness and love. In her depths he perceived she was waiting for his answer.

"I was thinking, Um Nabeel. Just thinking."

"Surely," she continued, "you must have been thinking of the trip. Since the letter arrived, I have not been able to sleep."

"You miss the young ones... Well, of course, that's natural, wife."

"The young men and the young women, light of my eyes. Do you think I will live to see them?"

"You will, by God's grace. May His name be praised and exalted."

12

God's graces poured forth onto Radwan through the children's letter, but he felt that there was something missing.

He asked himself what this could be. He soon found it: it was a feeling deep inside, which had taken hold of him ever since the children left, a feeling that he was cut off forever with his wife in the most difficult days of their lives.

The young ones had taken with them their energy, their future, their very life force. If only one of them were here, only one, he would not have the burden of preparing for this trip. As for him, Radwan, he did not know where to start.

13

He used to run away from home whenever one of the young ones decided to leave. He used to go out to the field, to the olive groves, to the vineyards. He used to find a thousand reasons not to stay at home and watch the preparations for the trip.

That was why he was completely in the dark as to the steps he should take.

He remembered, among other things, the night his eldest son, Nabeel, left them. Um Nabeel went with him to Beirut while he, Radwan, remained home.

"What would you call these actions other than cowardice?" he asked himself. "Admit it, man, and enjoy torturing yourself... Yes, you're a coward."

On that day he had said to Um Nabeel, "You are educated, you know how to go about things in the city. As for me, travel upsets me, and so does Beirut. I don't know how to get about in its streets crowded with people and cars."

Beirut still annoyed him, to this very hour. Memory took him back to that night when the eldest of his children was ripped out of his heart and the first of the rosary beads came loose.

On that day, he felt the house become empty. Darkness fell over the paths and the open areas of the village. All movement stopped, and even the winds subsided and took refuge in hidden tunnels.

He went to bed early, broken-hearted and downcast.

He tried to sleep after smoking too many hand-made cigarettes.

But how could he sleep.

His pillow was all thorns.

His mattress was a block of ice.

His heart beat in a way he could not describe.

Finally, he surrendered to sleep in the last part of that night.

It was not sleep but some kind of dark delirium that drowned him in a sea of nightmares. It was as if he was in a deep coma.

That's the best description of what happened to him. When he woke up in the morning, his pillow was wet.

All night, his pillow had been drinking his tears while he was unconscious.

In this state, his tears ran and ran.

He got up and walked with heavy steps. He carried the pillow and put it in the sun. He put on his clothes and went out to the field.

14

Um Nabeel was eager to travel and, like her, Radwan deeply missed every feature of the children's faces. But he would not weep now.

He would face reality with strength, with all the vigor and manliness he could command. He would not be a coward. He would not stay behind. Life was turning and the sun was about to set. If he did not seize this opportunity, he might not be given another.

From inside the house his wife's voice interrupted his thoughts.

"I heard that Simaan Al-Abras is going to Canada. Go and ask him, perhaps we can travel with him."

A great thought!

Um Nabeel always provided him with practical and helpful ideas.

Why did it not occur to him that Simaan was also traveling and in the same direction? The mukhtar of their village had told him so when he went to ask for a residence certificate.

Simaan, who worked in Beirut, knew the ins and outs. And, more important than that, he knew how to speak with the Consul.

He answered his wife enthusiastically, "A great suggestion, Um Nabeel. Simaan is clever and he's a good person. I'll go see him and discuss the matter with him."

15

He hurried through the narrow alleys of the village, treading softly on the ground lest he harm the grains of soil.

He used to walk along these familiar streets without the burning feeling that now possessed him.

Suddenly he felt waves of strange tenderness that flowed from his heart, welled up in his eyes and ran down in tears. He felt he was attached to everything he saw and heard: the tree that was turning from the freshness of summer to the yellow of autumn, the grey stones of the houses (he even thought he knew the number of stones in each house), the faces of the children playing in the curving lanes and the alley-ways. Even the atoms of dust flying around him and settling on his shoes were as dear as gold.

He raised his eyes to the sky now patched with the first signs of autumn, and his sight remained suspended there for a moment, fixed on the edge of a cloud moving hurriedly to the North.

These familiar scenes and paths were planted in his heart, painted on the retina of his eyes. And now he was going to leave them.

Here he was, looking for a traveling companion, willingly and consciously. He was going to travel.

He cringed at the thought.

"But I will return," he assured the stone walls of his village. "I am going for a short time and I will return. There is no need for all this sadness, no need for this confusion and anguish."

He said the last words aloud as he knocked at Simaan's door. The younger man welcomed Radwan and invited him in for coffee.

"We heard you are going on a trip, Simaan?"

"Yes, indeed, Uncle Radwan. When the papers arrive, we will go together to Beirut to collect them."

Simple words that took away the heavy burden on his shoulders and opened up the gate of hope.

"May God bless you and give you long life, my son."

16

A week passed during which the Consul's letter kept moving in Radwan's hands. He would examine it carefully, fold it up, give it to his wife and take it back from her, remembering what Simaan had translated for him:

"Please present yourself to the Canadian Consul's office in Beirut. The appointment is at eleven o'clock on the second day of September."

It just so happened that Simaan's appointment was on the same day. "Matters have been made simple, Um Nabeel," Radwan said in a jolly voice. "Quite simple. The Consul has asked me to represent you and act on your behalf."

17

His mission successfully accomplished, he went out carrying the visas and the two stamped passports. He walked with Simaan, shoulder to shoulder, so he would not lose him if he was a step behind. He was afraid to be lost in the wavy crowds, in this noise strange to his ears, in the mixture of clothes worn by men and women that made them look to him like clowns.

He laughed to himself, wonder showing on his forehead and in his blinking eyes. His laughter was suddenly replaced by anxiety when they arrived at a road block where several armed men stood.

"Simaan!" he whispered, placing his palm on his companion's shoulder.

Simaan understood Radwan's fear and calmed him in a low voice. "Don't be afraid, Uncle Radwan. The young men are here for security reasons."

"Weapons don't frighten me, you know," Radwan said. "It is the look in their eyes. I thought everyone said, two rounds and the war will be over. Ha! Beirut remains the city of surprises."

18

They then went to a travel agent to make reservations. Radwan followed his companion silently, submissively.

He had no way out. Going on the trip had become certain. The ax was approaching the base of the tree, and the tree was unable to escape.

He turned his thinking to the brighter side and saw the faces of his children and grandchildren looking at him from behind years of emigration and alienation, looming from color photographs of all sizes.

19

The office was crowded with people, all of whom wanted to travel.

They stood in line, most of them young men. They carried papers and waited. Radwan looked around searching for a grey-haired head like his, but was disappointed. The would-be emigrants were all young.

Suddenly, he felt that what he heard on the radio—and from those returning from Beirut to the village—was happening in front of his eyes: there was the beginning of war in Beirut. It made no difference whether two or three rounds were over.

Young men did not emigrate in times of peace and stability. And it did not appear that they were leaving to go on a visit.

He read the signs of war in their anguished faces and unsteady eyes. He suddenly missed his own children and could no longer bear being so far from them. Let them hurry and make a reservation for him so that he might travel. Please let them hurry! He stood in line and waited for what seemed an eternity. Simaan stood in front of him like a shield. Eventually, the younger man did all that was necessary. He reserved seats for three passengers on an airplane leaving Beirut in seven days.

20

"Praise be to God, wife. We've returned in safety." He greeted Um Nabeel as he got out of the taxi.

She was waiting for him at the outside gate, her eyes full of expectation.

"Everything is ready. Prepare yourself. We leave in a week."

Travel was always a surprise. Although she expected such news, she could not get used to the idea. She began to mutter, "In a week? In a week?"

Then she jumped up with the agility of a young woman and cried, chanted, "O apples of my eye, wait for me!"

21

The children chose for them to travel by air.

He would have preferred to travel by sea.

That was not because he had had experience traveling by sea but because of the idea. People had always traveled by sea, even in ancient times.

His brothers, Yusef and Saad, and his sister, Adla, had left before the First World War.

They left when he was only eight years old. He could not picture their faces now, but he did remember their names from fragments of stories that his mother had often repeated before she passed away.

His brothers and sister had been in the prime of youth.

Conditions at home had been ones of poverty and suffering. The earth grew only thorny bushes.

And they left. The brothers and sister no longer thought of their homeland after their parents died during the First World War.

His son Nabeel traveled by sea, and so did Hassan later.

When Jameel's turn came, travel by air had become available and it was much quicker.

Yet, the sea filled him with awe.

"O Sea, calm down your waves.

Our loved ones are in your cradle."

He thought of part of a *mejana* song which the mothers at Jurat Al-Sindyan repeated from the depths of their hearts as though the loved ones were ever roving the waves and were always traveling, never to set foot on land.

"O Sea, calm down your waves.

Our loved ones are in your cradle."

22

The airplane swayed as it moved, like a ship floating in space.

His seat was near a window, a window that connected him to the universe...to the highest limit the eye could reach.

His heart shivered at the thought that he was suspended between heaven and earth.

What if some mechanical trouble should befall the engines?

He quickly chased that idea from his mind, and called on his faith. "I trust in You, Omnipotent Power of the universe."

Then he turned to check on his wife. He found her sleeping.

Um Nabeel was good-hearted. Anxiety showed just around the edges of her eyes, he thought, but her face was softened by her faith and peaceful nature.

But how could she sleep on the airplane? He could not even close his eyes. He reviewed the reel of moving pictures stored in his memory. He took pleasure in recalling all that had happened since he had awakened that morning.

23

They had gathered to say good-bye to him.

This time, he was the one who was departing.

Lifetime friends. Men and women.

The old, the children.

They came to his house at dawn. Some of them asked him to convey their love and greetings to their loved ones. Others brought him bundles of different sizes and contents: pounded thyme with sesame seeds and sumac, pine nuts, raisins, dry figs, dry sour milk chunks...

He did not refuse any of their requests. His suitcases were full and about to burst, but he could not reject anything.

He knew what a handful of thyme meant when culled from the wilds of Jurat Al-Sindyan, pounded by affectionate hands, and filled with a mother's loving care.

He knew what the taste of pine nuts from the enduring pine trees on the Eastern hills meant to the immigrants in that unknown distant country.

And likewise, the dry figs and raisins which still preserved the fragrance of summer with its abundant sunshine.

He had finished packing his suitcases and was saying good-bye to the neighbors and relatives when he saw Crazy Roseanna standing at the door with a little bundle in her hand.

The sight of Roseanna always used to make him laugh.

He had often teased her on purpose in order to listen to her absurd ramblings. Sometimes she heaped insults on his head and anyone else who taunted her in order to strike up bizarre conversations.

Now, he was not smiling and he had no desire to tease Roseanna.

He tried to guess what the woman was carrying, and to whom she could be sending the gift. She had no relatives to remember and she lived alone in a hut resembling a hermit's cell, cut off from the world and its inhabitants. She only went out to disturb the peace and quiet of the villagers.

"What are you carrying, Roseanna?" he asked seriously. "Thyme or anise?"

The woman did not answer. She took two steps forward, then cupped her palms around the little bundle as she gave it to him.

"A handful of soil. I gathered it from the vineyard overlooking the valley. Take it to the young ones, Abu Nabeel. I thought the young ones might miss the scent of the soil of Jurat Al-Sindyan."

24

This woman was crazy, really crazy.

He looked around for someone to be a witness to this strange event. His well-wishers were occupied with Um Nabeel in the guest-room. He was alone with the suitcase.

Did Roseanna guess that he would be alone, and so chose the time and place to corner him thus? Or was it a coincidence, a mere coincidence?

But his heart beat a tune different from that of his mind. He felt that his chest was being squeezed, as though Roseanna's words were spearheads that penetrated his ribs and hit the most sensitive part of his soul.

A handful of soil!

He would carry it from Jurat Al-Sindyan to Charlottetown and present it as a gift to his children! What would their reaction be?

What would they say?

He raised his eyes to the woman and saw her standing firmly in her place, waiting for him to open his suitcase and add her gift to the others already crammed in.

And that was what he did. It was as if she had cast a magic spell on him which took him out of his normal self, stopped his logical thinking, kindling his emotion alone. What power this woman had!

He used to think she was crazy. The villagers had labelled her as a lunatic. He tried to rescue himself from the heavy atmosphere between him and her eyes.

"Your gift is the most precious one of all, Roseanna. I hope we will return in safety. I shall bring you back a worthwhile gift from the young ones."

"All I wish is your safety, Abu Nabeel."

She said these words, then turned her back, satisfied that she had accomplished her task.

She did not linger to say good-bye to Um Nabeel, and she ignored the babble of the children standing in the courtyard, ever-present witnesses to every event that took place in the village.

She turned her back and hastened away as she always did, turning neither left nor right. He continued to follow her with his eyes until she disappeared behind the twisting path that led to her hut.

He locked the suitcase and stood for a few moments thinking.

Finally he made a decision. I will tell nobody, he thought, not even Um Nabeel, about what Roseanna brought.

Deep inside he felt the place where no falsehood existed. The woman had shown a wisdom that was far superior to those in full possession of their faculties. A handful of soil! How many symbols within Roseanna's handful of soil!

25

The sound of a car horn brought Radwan back to reality.

The sound was like the fall of the curtain between two acts of a play.

The commotion that had subsided a few minutes earlier returned. Well-wishers spread out between the door and the garden, and a group of them surrounded the car.

The children rushed to carry the suitcases and bags. Um Nabeel was moving from a neighbor's shoulder to a friend's saying her good-byes, wiping her tears and unconsciously mumbling traditional words.

He maintained his composure, smiling to avoid the tears. He occupied himself with petty matters to distract his mind from the dramatic scene, until he got into the back seat of the car next to Um Nabeel. Simaan sat in the front.

"Go in peace and safety, neighbors." Um Said's voice, louder than all the others, spoke for everyone the traditional good wishes which had often been repeated in this open space. "A thousand good wishes for your safe trip."

The voice echoed in his ears and the world turned into a cloud. Heavy fog descended like a curtain, screening off the outside from his sight. And his tears ran down.

He wiped them furtively, swallowing the lump in his throat. To get rid of it, he reminded himself of what was waiting for him on the other side of the globe, of the beloved faces implanted there.

26

The car wound through the paths. His eyes leapt in all directions trying to store up an image from every vineyard, terrace and grazing ground. The images racing before his eyes were in color, embroidered with the shy morning rays of the September sun.

In a few minutes, the car crossed the lands of Jurat Al-Sindyan and entered the boundaries of the neighboring villages. There loomed the houses of Hasbaya, an ancient town with buildings older than memory. Its quiet houses with their red tile roofs made it look like they were firmly rooted to the ground as though they had been there forever.

How many friends he had in this town!

But he had no time to stop and say good-bye.

To a flock of pigeons flying above the houses, he called, "We'll meet when I return...God willing!"

As the car crossed the marketplace of Hasbaya, he raised both hands in greeting to every face he knew and to every look that silently asked, Where are you going?

To Canada. Yes, I am going to Canada.

He wished he could put his head out of the car window and spread the news so that everybody would know!

"I'm going to Charl'ton... Just a short visit to the young ones, then I'll return with Um Nabeel. Yes, we will return."

He repeated the same sentence when the car passed a group of armed men stationed at the Hasbani River crossroads.

The young men smiled. They understood the situation. In unison they yelled, "A happy and safe trip!"

27

The reel of pictures rolled on in his consciousness.

The Hasbani River and its silvery waterfall disappeared from sight.

How often he had sat there on the floating docks!

How many pleasant nights of joy and happiness were stored up in his memory!

Pain squeezed his heart as he saw the park empty and the docks destroyed. This fountain of abundance, the groves of pomegranates, olive, apple and quince trees, had become the victims of bombardment and destruction.

In the last raid launched by the Israeli planes, incendiary bombs called napalm bombs were used and, later, cluster bombs came too.

What shame grape clusters must have felt at this name!

A napalm bomb burnt the grove of his younger brother, Naaman. In addition to his trees, he had lost his herd of sheep and cows. If it were not for God's grace, he would have lost his life as well, for the fire reached his shirt and the bottom of his trousers.

And how many children were victims of cluster bombs!

How many songs were silenced, songs that used to rise from the shepherds and their reed flutes which echoed through the groves and the hills.

But that was long ago.

Now he was being whisked away from these precious places nestling in his heart.

28

Again he consoled himself with the idea that he would not be away for long, and that the absence of one person did not make much difference.

Then he stopped short.

Yes. The absence of one person *did* make a difference. The absence of one person might trigger another's. That was what had happened to his children. In the beginning, it was Nabeel who left. Radwan had thought that the others who still remained at home would take his place. Then Nabeel began inviting them, one by one, and they accepted the invitations in spite of their father and even in spite of what they felt in their hearts.

There was an invisible power that threatened them and their future, and lured them into the belief that going away from their homeland was part of man's nature and this adventure could improve their lives. Then they would return in a few years to cultivate the land and renovate the houses.

A few years! The number now was twenty.

And life passed... Life was still passing.

The houses were still in the same condition they had been when they left. The number of deserted homes was increasing year after year. The proportion of wasteland was rising. And the young men continued to follow the route to the West.

It was a tragedy!

He understood its meaning...he, Um Nabeel, Um Said and all the neighbors and friends who rushed to say farewell to them that morning.

Even Roseanna, in her seclusion, was conscious of the problem and stretched out her hand to the earth to gather a handful of soil and send a gift to the young ones, as though it were the last call for help from a land on fire.

29

Was the land really burning?

What was happening to his homeland?

He asked himself these questions again and again, even as he got out of the car and walked with Simaan and Um Nabeel among the dense crowds of the airport.

Beirut International Airport: the network which connected his homeland to the world.

A place of endless activity.

From here, people traveled to the farthest corners of the world.

Three of his children had left him at these gates. And now, the airport was crowded with young men.

He felt that these young men resembled the ones who had stood in line with him at the Canadian Consulate and at the travel agent's office. The face of one of them was repeated in ten or even a hundred faces.

They were almost all of similar height and color, and their eyes were filled with anxiety.

"What do you think, Simaan? Are all these people leaving?"

And Simaan, who worked in Beirut, tried to give a soothing answer.

"Yes, most of them, Uncle Radwan. Those within the gate are leaving, but those outside have come to bid them farewell."

"God bless them, God bless them!"

He wanted to ask Simaan another question, to relieve the sudden fear which overtook him and ran through his veins, sending a cold shiver through his body.

"Is this a new phenomenon? Or has this always been the state of affairs?"

It was as though Simaan had read his thoughts or felt instinctively that his earlier response was incomplete. So he said, "The situation is still unsatisfactory, Uncle Radwan. Two rounds of the war have ended, but there are predictions..."

"And what do the predictions say? What do people in Beirut think?"

"Most conversations revolve around the next war. People are pessimistic, and those who are able to leave do not hesitate."

30

Indeed, he was able to leave, but he had neither chosen the trip nor the timing. It was the young ones who chose. This trip was their choice.

They finished at the airline counter and went through security, ending up in the departing hall.

He could not believe what he saw: people lying on the floor, sleeping on suitcases, bags and blankets.

He looked around to find a seat for Um Nabeel. But how would he find such a seat? Where would a man find a resting place for his head these days?

It was like the Day of Resurrection. The scene brought tears to his eyes.

In all his life, he had never seen people so resigned. It was as though they had placed themselves in Fate's hands.

His own fate was an airplane that was due to take off in a few minutes and save him from this horror.

And what did he see?

If he was able to read, he could have perhaps studied the newspapers and better understood what was going on.

If he was able to read, he would not have been satisfied with the drone of the radio, nor would he have bothered Simaan with his many questions. If...

But the word "if" came too late. For a voice announced, above the din, the imminent departure of his flight to London.

31

"How the world has changed, Simaan!"

Radwan's words were spoken over his wife's head.

Simaan had just finished reading the newspaper and placed it in the pocket in front of his seat. He prepared himself for lunch and asked Radwan to pull down the little table in front of him. Um Nabeel followed suit.

"It's lunchtime," Simaan told them.

"How the world has changed, Simaan!" Radwan repeated. He could not conceal his surprise at what he saw and heard. Signs of wonder had showed on his forehead and in his eyes ever since he had climbed the stairs to the airplane and fastened his seatbelt. He put himself in the flight captain's hands and resigned himself to the whim of Fate.

And here they were now, preparing his lunch. This was an event he would tell the neighbors about back home — if Fate spared him, that is.

He would tell them, "I'm telling you, friends, we are living in an amazing, strange world. When had man ever dreamed of flying, of overtaking eagles in the air? He not only flies like birds, but also sits comfortably while flying and is served by beautiful and pleasant young women. He gives them orders and they obey."

He thought, what more could I ask for?

Nothing.

His desires had all vanished and he had no wish to ask for anything. He was content to sit, just like that, comfortable in his seat. He was suspended between heaven and earth, looking from the window and feeling that he could reach out and touch the edges of the universe with his fingertips. On top of all that, they were serving him drinks and a delicious lunch. What an amazing world today's world was!

What other strange things could possibly be lying ahead of him?

He took the tray from the hostess and put it firmly on the table in front of him. He asked Um Nabeel to do likewise, then they both fell silent as though they were performing a worship ritual.

32

That was how he appeared on the outside.

But on the inside, his world was in turmoil. It was as if there was a kettle in his chest, simmering and then boiling over.

At times he was ecstatic, but most of the time he was simply bewildered.

He had been turned into a child who was just entering the world of adults to face an unfolding universe that was inviting him to gaze.

In all his life, which had spanned seventy years, he had seen nothing of the world but that small spot, Jurat Al-Sindyan and its immediate surroundings. The longest trip he had ever taken was to Beirut. Fear was his shadow whenever he was obliged to go to that amazing city. He never got used to its noise, its hustle and bustle, the fast traffic of its crowded streets, the dialect of its people.

He had never allowed his imagination to leap from the earth and fly to dizzying heights, where a winged silver machine soared through the blue sky, gently disturbing the tranquillity and shining like an unreachable star.

Planes had rarely passed over Jurat Al-Sindyan; the village was not on the regular flight path. So they remained an enigma which he did not dare think about or imagine.

Then suddenly everything had changed and the silent dialogue between him and what he thought was a gentle dove came to an abrupt end.

One day...

33

He remembered it now.

He remembered it well.

It was an ordinary September day.

He had prepared himself for a hunting trip.

It was one of the many trips in which he had foraged on the slopes of Mount Hermon.

He gathered around him his companions for the trip: Stella, his hunting dog; Sricca, the deceitful female partridge that he kept in a cage to lure the males with her tender cooing; Dusty, his donkey; and the double-barreled shotgun which was his mate on desolate paths.

Everything was as he had known it for half a century. The wind-
ing, stony path, which he traveled with Dusty, had not changed for
centuries and continued to wind upwards among the narrow mountain trails worn down by the donkeys ever since humans had do-
mesticated the animal.

Dusty carried a saddlebag on his back inflated with empty baskets. The orchards of the mountain pass were heavy with fruit that
season. He had assured Um Nabeel that he would return with baskets overflowing with the orchard's treasures.

And up there, at the foot of Mount Hermon where he could reach
out his finger and touch the clouds, Radwan improvised his hunting barricade.

Little gaps among the jagged rocks provided a good peephole
for his gun. He began to camouflage them with terebinth and worm-
wood branches.

From this fortress he could observe the partridges as they vied
with one another to reach Sricca, who wooed the unknown knights
of her dreams, singing to them of desolation, loneliness and loss,
and stretching out to them melodious paths that led the poor males
astray.

He laughed in secret when he thought of Sricca's trick. He could
not help comparing her with humans, for women acted much the
same. He was about to curse their gender, but then he remembered
Um Nabeel. She had been beside him all her life, a model of loyalty,
love and sacrifice. No, no. Her name was sacred and he did not allow himself to put her on the same level as other women.

Um Nabeel was a princess among women, the mother of his
young ones.

How easily man's thinking could be distracted!

What a dark world the human heart was!

34

He returned to his surrounding and heard again the cooing of Sricca
coming from the cage that hung from the branch of an ancient fig
tree.

He crouched, doing his best to keep his head level with the peephole through which he aimed his gun. He sat there waiting.

Quiet reigned all around him. It was a velvety kind of quiet
dappled by the rays of the sun.

Not a sound could be heard in the area, nothing but the tunes of Sricca cooing freely, then the echoes returning from the valley. The waves of her passionate call reached the birds flying about in the pine hills. Partridges began to arrive from all directions.

He waited until the whole flock was within range, and then he fired.

The explosion sounded as if it were the first one in history. It shattered the tranquillity, and the frightened birds flew away hysterically.

Except for the unlucky.

Stella leapt like a tiger and brought the game to him. He took pleasure counting them: one, two, three.

He had hit three partridges with one shot. Sricca was silent.

Giving Sricca an opportunity to examine her conscience, he got up to pluck some grapes from the vines and filled the first basket. He then took his hooked cane, an azarole stick that he used to bend down the high fig tree branches, and began picking the honeyed fruits, arranging them neatly in the second basket.

After a few minutes of silent picking the two baskets were full. He stuffed the three partridges in his knapsack, which hung from the trunk of the fig tree. He returned to the barricade to try his luck once more.

He waited until the captive inside of the cage had forgotten her deed. She then began to sing, hesitantly at first, but soon she sang without interruption as if she were telling the hills and mountains the greatest story of all in which she was the principal character.

He waited a few minutes but no birds showed.

He began to think that the male gender was superior to the female in intelligence and cleverness — at least among the birds... Remembering his daughter, Nawal, he did not allow himself to continue with this thought. She had reached a level of knowledge which her brothers had not, causing him to change many of his earlier theories about women. Nawal was now a university professor. And there, in Canada, only God knew where her ambition would take her.

He would meet her shortly and see for himself how far she had gone. Ten years of separation had blurred his vision. He could not see her clearly. He could not distinctly remember or imagine her face, her movements, her smile, her ready wit.

Curse the time! Curse the separation from the homeland!

Yet, even if he forgot all his past, he would never forget how his hunting trip ended that day...

The male partridges hesitated to come near. The trick would not fool them again, at least for this day. The female partridge sang her heart out, calling and extending her throat to the limit. The sun was getting warmer and its rays were refracted through the molecules of dry air, spreading warmth throughout his body. He felt his skin was part of its generosity.

He got up and loaded the two baskets on Dusty. He then called Stella, who at once was at his side, wagging her tail with a sense of joy and victory. Deep in his heart, he felt the same. He led Dusty down the path.

Suddenly he heard a roaring boom. At first it sounded like thunder, but the sky was clear and there were no clouds.

The thundering boom grew louder, almost deafening. And then...

O Lord!

What he saw...

A squadron of airplanes, as big as eagles, crossing the sky with the speed of lightning, and swooping down like thunderbolts on Jurat Al-Sindyan, his precious village!

He stood watching the scene from that height, not believing his eyes... He saw three airplanes dive to the level of the low roofs and others form an air cover for them. (This was the expression he heard on the radio: air cover.) Earlier they had bombarded the Hasbani fountainhead in this manner, and today they were reaching out to his village. The roaring of the planes was drowned by the violent explosions. They were bombing the houses, the peaceful earthen homes, and the red-tile roofs that decorated the village. Clouds of smoke billowed in the air. The airplanes then swerved upward and his eyes followed them until they disappeared beyond the southern horizon.

He had heard tell of their aggression and their terrorizing raids on the southern villages. But that was only hearsay. Once he had seen smoke rising behind the southern hill when they bombed Shwayya and Ain Qinya and the area nearby. Today they had reached Jurat Al-Sindyan.

The planes disappeared but the sound of the explosions continued to ring in his ears, accompanying him on his frantic journey home. His heart throbbed. He met no one on the road. He saw the smoke rising from several houses, including the house with the red-tile roof that faced his own.

"Where is Um Nabeel?" His thoughts were only of her. He pounded on the door.

She was not there. Nor were the neighbors in any of their houses. They had all taken refuge on the ground floor of their neighbor's house, Jameel al-Duri's, which was the only one in the neighborhood that had two floors.

He quickly unloaded the donkey and placed the baskets in the front hall of his own house. Then he ran towards Jameel's where he beheld a scene that would stay with him all his life: the people of his neighborhood huddled in a heap in a dark corner, the women, the men, the disabled, the children. . .their faces were frozen, their eyes protruded, their tongues were tied—except for those of the children who were screaming in terror.

He did not greet them with the usual words of peace. He did not utter a single word. He stretched out his hand to Um Nabeel, pulling her up from the tile floor where she crouched. He led her home, murmuring, "Thank God for your safety! Thank God you are safe!"

Many hours passed before the others dared to return to their homes. Their return was accompanied by this new and painful memory that would never be absent from their minds again, day or night.

And thus, everything changed. Days lost their usual flavor. The silent dialogue between him and the gentle dove ended when he saw the dove abandon gentleness and turn into a hawk that carried out blitzing raids, destroyed peaceful homes, and killed residents rooted in the earth like the olive trees.

A long time passed before he was able to distinguish the difference between airplanes that carried people and goods and airplanes that carried the destruction of human beings.

But for Um Nabeel, she still grasped his arm whenever she heard a roaring boom. And she would repeat, "Lord, forgive us! Lord, have mercy on us!"

Now she was embarrassed to show her fear as she sat comfortably in this soft seat, waited on by young women who were like the houris of paradise. Simaan was next to her explaining everything so that he had almost convinced her she was not flying but rather was sitting in a salon of an earthly guest house.

35

The houri returned to collect the empty plates, smiling at everyone. Radwan's eyes followed her movements, thinking she was smiling for him alone. Her radiant smile penetrated the depths of his soul, spreading warmth and reassurance.

"Praise be to the Creator!" he said to Simaan unabashedly. "What beauty!"

The hostess had gone to another section where she continued to assist and smile at the other passengers.

Simaan turned to him. "You haven't seen anything yet, Uncle Abu Nabeel. This is only the beginning of the trip...."

36

But the trip from Beirut to London was coming to an end.

In Arabic, an invisible voice announced from an invisible place, "Ladies and gentlemen. In a few minutes we will be landing at Heathrow Airport. Please, fasten your seatbelts, extinguish all cigarettes and remain in your seats. We wish you a happy stay in London."

His ears, like a radar device, picked up every signal and not a single word escaped them. Radwan felt a little disturbed at these last words.

"Are we going to stay in London?" he whispered to Simaan.

With a smile Simaan reassured him. "That is only an expression, Uncle Radwan. For some passengers the trip will end in London. The others go to airplanes which will take them to their destinations. The others, that is us."

"You have reassured me, my son. You know, one must be all eyes and ears, and should not let a single word escape, otherwise ...."

"Otherwise what?" Um Nabeel asked anxiously, who, until then, had kept her peace.

Radwan let loose a mocking laugh that made his mustaches dance.

By the time the wheels of the plane had touched the runway, he had regained his composure and confidence. The plane taxied with the grace and freedom of the partridges above the slopes of Mount Hermon.

But were the partridges of Mount Hermon still free? And was this airplane really as free as he thought, or were there bounds and limits?

37

Man poses questions with every footstep that leads him along new paths.

Radwan's future path stretched out beyond the range of his sight. His present path was unpaved and was leading him into the jungles of Western civilization, into an unfamiliar world, into the New World.

He and his wife moved towards the other plane that would take them across the Atlantic Ocean. They tacitly followed Simaan who knew how to read the signs and the monitors announcing flight departures.

They had no time to rest or look around Heathrow Airport.

Simaan was the leader and they both followed. He knew how to speak English.

They went to the ticket counter to confirm their reservations. Then the three of them found their departure gate.

Like the jaws of an extinct mythical beast, the door was wide open, swallowing people up at the signal of the hostesses who stood like guardian angels: one on the right and the other on the left.

How comforting were their angelic smiles!

How they alleviated one's anxieties and apprehensions!

Radwan was surprised at how smoothly everything was going. He was not afraid as he had been at the Consulate, and this surprised him. He was following the herd being led to its destiny.

He had not realized how large the airplane was until he was inside and had taken his seat in a middle row.

"Is this an airplane, Simaan, or is it a mountain?"

"A jet, Uncle Radwan, a jumbo jet."

"What did you say? Janbu?"

"Jumbo, that's its name. It takes four hundred passengers or more. We are in the lower deck, and there is an upper deck too."

"Blessed be the name of God. Does that mean there are people above us?"

"Yes, there are many people above us.

"And here I was thinking that there was nothing above us except the face of thy Exalted and Almighty Lord."

He then turned to Um Nabeel to reassure her.

"Rejoice, Um Nabeel, rejoice. You are traveling to Canada in a two-floor building. We have spent all our lives in Jurat Al-Sindyan, living in a one-floor building. Who could ever dream of such a great treat?"

Um Nabeel answered enthusiastically, "May God bless those who were the cause.... May He bring this trip to a good end."

"May God hear your prayer, wife," Radwan said as he followed Simaan's movements with his eyes. He saw him fasten his seatbelt, so he asked Um Nabeel to do likewise. He fastened his own and sat cheerfully, watching the action around him. He soon heard the roar of the engines.

The mountain was about to take off.

This giant of a structure would rise with its heavy load as if it were a house sparrow carrying no weight but the feathers of its wings.

The doors closed and the mountain moved. Between the roar outside and the hum of low voices inside, it took off.

And as an eagle would level its wings on reaching its highest altitude, the plane stabilized itself in the foggy space. Then it went on to cleave the veils of heaven, rising further and penetrating the dense and mysterious grey-white mountains of giant clouds.

His eyes were preoccupied watching the imaginary line of flight: the plane, doubtlessly, was moving in a certain line, but who could see that line or define it?

And, like a child, Radwan began to think anxiously, how was the airplane guided to its intended destination when there was no paved road and there were no clear directions?

He reached deep into his memory, hoping to uncover the mystery. He let the echoes hum and jabber in diverse languages around him. When he did not find the answer, he turned to Simaan.

"A mind-perplexing matter."

"What is the cause of your perplexity, Uncle Radwan?"

"The cause, my son, is this jumbo jet. How does it know its way among the clouds?"

Simaan encouraged him with a good-hearted smile. "The matter may be difficult for our thinking because we don't know the principles of aviation. As for the captain, the engineer and the experts, they find the matter extremely easy."

"Of course, it is easy for them. But I want to know this: does it never happen that an airplane leaves its specified line of direction?"

"That happens sometimes. But, in any event, its direction is not determined by a paved road. It is all done by pressing buttons and moving instruments under the control of the captain."

"I see. The matter is not easy, Simaan. The captain has concerns, too."

"You're perfectly right, Uncle Radwan. His concern for us is his responsibility, and our safety is in his hands."

"He must have a mountain of a brain, this captain."

"You've said it. The captain may not make an error. If it is permissible for him to err on the ground, it is not so in the sky."

"True, true..."

38

Radwan nodded, content with this amount of information, for he did not want to delve more deeply into the tunnels of the New World.

He had no wish to face its complexities.

He returned to his inner world, snuggling in its warmth and feeling protected from the cold and domination of this enormous outside world which contracted man's size and made him feel smaller than an ant.

Man, here, is an ant, he thought to himself. People congregate, walk in groups like ants, unknown in a world that does not know them or care for them.

In his village, man was still big. He still counted, from childhood until he reached old age. His place was still preserved in the hearts of his compatriots. Even death was unable to destroy that place at times.

In his village, man lived within the circle of his little world in dignity — honored and protected.

He, Radwan, had left this circle.

He was made to leave this sanctuary — was literally pushed into the outside world. He remembered a similar exodus at the beginning of his life.

39

He was a child. He had not yet left the warmth of human laps when the war broke out.

Now they called it the First World War. In those days it was just the War; that is, famine, sickness, living life a fugitive, the abandonment of warm laps.

His father and mother did not survive the horrors. They succumbed in the first round. The war crushed them and he was left behind with two brothers and a sister, the eldest of whom was no more than fourteen.

His three older siblings, who had emigrated many years before, remained mere names in his memory: Adla, Saad and Yusef.

He tried to recall their faces, but his imagination failed him.

What is the use, Radwan, he asked himself. They did not care for you. When you and your siblings were like baby chicks, they abandoned you and did not ask about you.... Or do you think they asked but their letters were lost?

What is the difference? In any case, no one had heard from them and thus the four younger children had entered the miserable world of orphans: they tramped about the streets, were homeless at night, and they toiled in the service of others.

They were tossed hither and yon, pawns of the nouveaux riches who had profited from the war. These people had exploited their childhood, their misery and homelessness. The children had slaved for every meal.

How hard they had had to work for that meal!

In spite of all that, they grew up. They rooted their childhood to the banks of the Hasbani River, whose generous water had nourished their roots and quenched their thirst, exactly as it quenched that of the poplars, the sycamores and the willows...and the bountiful orchards where pomegranates, quinces, apples and olives grew.

When adolescence bloomed in their beautiful eyes, they stayed close to the Hasbani breast. Faris, the oldest among them, became a partner of a big landowner whose agricultural possessions he managed for one-fourth the produce.

As for Fareedeh, she was fortunate to marry early, by the grace of God.

He, Radwan, took over with his younger brother, Naaman, the running of a watermill belonging to Fayez Bey al-Hasbani.

Miller.

That was his job. Naaman helped him: he unloaded the wheat and bulghur sacks from the animals' backs to be ground or crushed, then helped the clients load them afterwards. The clients came from the neighboring villages extending from Rashawa and Wadi-t-Taym to Marji'yoon. The food of all the region, from the foot of Mount Hermon to the farthest limit of Mount Amel, passed between his arms and those of his brother Naaman.

The work was not without hardship. But it afforded them many blessings: earning a living and a surplus, getting to know people and make friends with them. The mill was a place of work but it was also a center where the people of the villages met, where they exchanged news, and where they sometimes spent their evenings in pleasant conversation.

A broad smile spread in his heart when he remembered those days, when one's mind was at rest and one's stomach free from hunger.... He was then in the prime of his youth.

And not all of his customers were men.

In spite of the dangers of travel, young women of breathtaking beauty used to come to him from time to time. They used to reduce the cheerlessness of the place and the deprivation of the heart. He would content himself in these meetings with a wink or a meaningful smile which would spread shyness like blushing roses on the cheeks of the girls. Sometimes he would dare utter a flirting word or an amusing anecdote that would bring him closer to the sweet transient girl and leave behind it a smattering of yearning, desires, memories and even promises of another quick meeting in the very near future.

40

This was his world, until, one day, a young woman so different from the others came to him. She was tall and slender, had a graceful walk and was gentle, pretty and shy.

"How beautiful you were in your youth, Um Nabeel!"

He turned to the woman occupying the seat next to him, who was relaxing in a blissful nap.

"You were and still are beautiful," he whispered.

But, that morning...

He sat up in his seat, shut off all the sounds around him, dispelled all scenes and faces in order to concentrate on her image with all his senses.

Her face was as bright as a velvety rose opening up on a spring morning. Her eyes were like merry butterflies of a green and honey color in which joy and good-heartedness entwined, fluttering around him, penetrating his eyelashes, and overpowering his resistance...

He did not dare approach her and speak with her as he did with other young women. She was surrounded by a group of people from her own village.

From what village?

He did not need to ask. He knew them. They were his customers and he knew them. They were from Jurat Al-Sindyan, the village whose houses were spread between the pine hills and the olive hills.

"Whose daughter is she?" he asked the elder of the group in passing, so that his question would appear spontaneous and far from any ulterior motive.

The man replied, "This is Raya, daughter of Tawfeeq Abu Nijim. Her brothers left for New York and she remained alone with her parents. Her father sent her with us so that she would get used to the work."

"You mean, she is the man of the house." He tried to be nonchalant.

The elder nodded.

"My son," he said, "emigration swallows the men. And the women remain behind to guard the homes and the agricultural lands. Because of the rulers, our young men are forced to flee. People sell their properties in order to buy the ship fare and save their children from the injustices of the system... Every family has planted a seedling or more in the new land, a land of alienation, and that's not the end of it..."

The man's words struck Radwan deep in his heart.

Every family had planted a seedling or more. His own family had planted three seedlings in the new land.

What had become of those seedlings?

If only someone would tell him, one day!

If only someone would let him know about his brothers and sister!

41

Digging into the depths of his memory for her beautiful image, he saw her lifting the sack, his brother Naaman opposite her helping load it onto her donkey. He ran to give her a hand.

"The arms of young women have not been created to carry burdens. Let me do it for you."

"Working is not a shameful thing," she answered in a sweet, resonant voice. "The women of our village are equal partners with men."

"There's no doubt about that," he said. "I can see you are a prime example! God be with you."

She drove the donkey and walked along with the group. He remained transfixed, his eyes following her, his heart throbbing. A question boiled inside him. "Will she return, I wonder?"

Would his eyes behold her again soon?

When he returned to his millstone, her face kept flashing in his mind, distracting him. Her voice reverberated above the din: "Working is not a shameful thing."

His humble job, then, would not be considered shameful. If he approached her, she would not turn away.

But what did he know about her family? What did he know about her father? Would the man receive him in his home if he were to visit, or would he kick him out, muttering, "A miller?! Marry my daughter to a miller? That's the last thing I would do!"

42

Her father was a landowner, like all the people in Jurat Al-Sindwan, like all the customers who brought the bountiful crops of their fields to his mill. In this society, a person was valued by the amount of land he owned.

Radwan had owned some property. His brother Faris had sold it when they had fallen on hard times after the War and almost died of hunger.

He was now eager to become a landowner again, to plant himself like an olive sapling in the good earth.

If he owned land, he would have followed Raya to her home, to the innermost part of her house. He would have sat with her father and spoken with him as an equal.

If only he was a landowner! The millstone was turning fast and its noisy grating brought him back to his senses. He hurried to carry out his customers' orders.

From that day forward, her face never left him. He burned with desire for her return with the people from Jurat Al-Sindyan.

43

Radwan waited, and his waiting was long.

Their meeting had been a turning point in his life, one that transformed his days and painted them in colors.

He began to move, talk and work as though he was always in her presence, as if her eyes were observing his every movement.

Deep inside he wondered if this could be love.

This feeling carried him away and cast him into places full of dreams. He struggled with reality but more often with illusions. He stood between two worlds, but didn't know if he should advance or retreat. Would reality or illusion win the battle?

44

Was this love?

He almost posed the question to a man who spoke to him about Raya one day. The man had come with a group from Jurat Al-Sindyan but Raya was not among the women.

"Where is she?" Radwan whispered in the man's ear. "One of your companions is missing."

"You mean Raya?" the man asked quietly.

"Yes."

He did not dare mention her name to the villagers. He was afraid the word would come out burning and scorch the eyes of the listener.

"Her family is small," he heard the man say. "One bag of flour lasts them two months. Why don't you visit us in Jurat Al-Sindyan, Radwan?"

Radwan cast a look of surprise at the man. Was he seriously inviting him? Or was he testing and trying to find out his secret?

What could he mean by his question?

Radwan became more cautious lest he utter a word that might hurt Raya or be wrongly interpreted. He swallowed his words, but they stayed like a lump in his throat.

The man urged him on. "The people of Jurat Al-Sindyan are your friends. You must visit us. You can be a guest in my house. My house is yours. Ask only for Abu Naji."

"May your house be forever prosperous, Uncle Abu Naji."

His answer was the usual, traditional one. But in his heart, there was a hopeful prayer that the man would continue.

Abu Naji came closer and whispered in his ear, "I'll introduce you to Tawfeeq Abu Nijim, Raya's father. He is one of the best people in our village."

Radwan stepped back a little, rooted to the spot, while the man's eyes focused intently on him as if to uncover his true feelings.

What would he say to him?

What would he answer him?

Could he ask for anything more than this?

Abu Naji did not seem to be a cheap gossiper. His invitation was sincere. He extended a friendly hand to Radwan, its deep furrows holding all the goodness of the earth and the fragrance of bountiful soil.

"May you remain ever well, Abu Naji."

45

Everything on his first trip to her village was filled with promise.

The day was one of those refreshing autumn ones. The sun had stopped its burning summer heat and was surrounded by a veil of clouds that left open some blue patches bringing joy to the soul. All along the way, the banks of the Hasbani River wore a new mantle embroidered with gold threads, adorned with rubies and emeralds.

Wonderful autumn colors!

The September birds conversed intimately on the tree branches and gathered in flocks exchanging secrets about their imminent migration to the South.

His own trip was to the East.

The peaks of Mount Hermon remained within range of his vision for a whole hour.

The road to Raya lay to the East. Her face was the sun that illuminated his life and brought him happiness.

On the day of their wedding, she outshone the sun as she was
led to him in the bridal procession.

"At the sight of your face, O jewel,
The sun stepped back abashed...."

Thus began the song chanted by the young men on his wedding
day.

He turned to the woman sitting peacefully next to him on the
plane.

"A rare jewel you are indeed, Um Nabeel. In your past and in
your present, you're a jewel. And what a jewel!"

46

Abu Naji received him warmly and treated him like an emigrant
son returning home. He made him sit in the place of honor in his
house, treated him hospitably to food and drink, and put him up in
the guest room. The following day he accompanied him to the house
of Tawfeeq Abu Nijim.

Raya's father was a man of venerable appearance. He had a
charming personality and a generous disposition. Radwan liked him
at first sight.

Raya's mother seemed to be good-hearted, but was reserved in
her conversation and behavior.

Raya did not hide or run away from his presence as was the
custom. Rather, she offered glasses of rose water to the two guests,
then disappeared, as the traditions of Jurat Al-Sindyan dictated.

There was no way to conceal the purpose of the visit. Abu Naji
expressed it in simple words:

"Sheykh Tawfeeq, we've come with a purpose. Radwan Abu
Yusef is not a stranger to us. The people of Jurat Al-Sindyan know
him: he's a good, industrious young man. He is now before you
requesting the honor of being related to your eminent family by
marriage."

Her father listened attentively in order to understand clearly all
that was being said. When the spokesman stopped, the father raised
his eyes to Radwan and asked him, "When did you meet my daughter?"

An extremely simple question. Yet to Radwan, it was as if he
had touched an electric wire. His cheeks reddened. His words came
out in a stutter.

"At the...well, at the mill...on the day she came with Abu Naji...and the people of the village."

"And this is sufficient for you to ask for her hand?" the father asked.

"I hope you think well of me."

"Give me some time to consult with the girl and her mother."

At these words, Abu Naji stood up to leave. Radwan followed him out, noticing the signs of promise in Sheykh Tawfeeq's eyes.

Radwan did not lack refinement or handsome looks. He was sensitive, considerate of others, very conscious of where his limits began and ended. He measured his words carefully. All this he did not learn at school, for he never went to school. He had learned it from his great teacher: life. He had learned it from continuous struggle, from living with nature, from contemplation of people's behavior.

He was endowed with a quick sense of understanding, with perception by intuition without resorting to words.

When they were both outside, Abu Naji turned to him.

"I see promising signs in this visit, Radwan, my son. Sheykh Tawfeeq is one of the most honored people in our village. He seeks a man of good character. And that is abundantly clear in you. Expect good news. I'll remain a messenger of peace between you both and I'll speak well of you about anything that I failed to express adequately in our first session."

Radwan said simply, "Please don't spice it up. Frankness is the foundation of a happy marriage."

"I will speak only of what I see in you."

47

Radwan's good qualities tipped the balance in his favor. Abu Naji came a week later with the good news.

"Congratulations. May God bring the joyful event to completion."

Radwan threw his arms around the man, leaving traces of flour on his clothes, which he began to brush off in embarrassment. He did not know what to do with himself. He rushed to the coffeepot, put it on the fire and invited his friend to drink coffee with him and continue the conversation.

"You'll have to visit the young woman's family again," Abu Naji said.

"I'd like to know Raya's opinion," Radwan said anxiously. "Is she willing?"

"You'll know that when you meet with her."

48

He met her several times during their period of engagement before the wedding. He learned that she harbored similar feelings towards him, and had done so since their first meeting. But a girl should not take the initiative.

A question remained, fluttering like a butterfly deep inside him. But his sense of modesty would not allow him to voice it.

He knew the economic and class distinctions that stood as barriers between people in little villages, often to the point of rejection and fanaticism. It could even become more severe toward strangers. Yes, he was a stranger and his economic position did not qualify him to be an in-law to this eminent family. Raya may have been above these matters, but why would her parents agree?

His question remained unasked — and unanswered — but his anxiety disappeared with the warm welcome he received whenever he visited Raya and her parents. He soon began to feel like he was a member of the family.

49

He had almost forgotten the old anxiety when one evening he was returning from a visit to his fiancée and came upon a strange woman who stood in his way.

He had said good-bye to Raya and her parents, got on his horse and had ridden towards the west. At the edge of the village he saw a woman wrapped in a cloak which hid everything except her head. She stood in the middle of the road.

He had never before seen this woman's face. She had a certain strange beauty. She was about thirty-five years of age, slender and tall and of white complexion.

"Good evening, young man," she greeted him.

"Good evening," he answered in surprise.

"I have a few words to say to you.... My name is Roseanna."

"I'm honored, Roseanna. Good news, I hope!"

"I congratulate you on your engagement. You are very fortunate. Forgive my ignorance, but what is your name?"

"Your servant Radwan, Radwan Abu Yusef."

"Congratulations, Radwan. You've come at the right time."

"I don't understand, Roseanna."

"If you had asked for Raya's hand two years ago, you would have been disappointed."

Her words aroused his curiosity. What had happened two years ago?

He asked her to go on, and she quickly answered, "I've said enough. Raya will tell you the rest."

His curiosity leapt like a barometer. She must have intended to continue her story, he thought, or else why would she have way-laid him in such a strange manner?

"No.... You started. Please, continue. What happened two years ago?"

"Two years ago, brother Radwan, Raya's sister Almas got married."

"And what is so strange about that?"

"They married her to a wealthy widower from America who had four children. Almas was eighteen and he was forty. Her immigrant brothers were furious. They wrote harsh words to their father, threatening to sever their relationship with the family if he married their sister to the man. But the father had given his word. And a word of honor cannot be broken. And so, Almas paid the price of the word 'yes' spoken by her father."

Radwan listened to the story, expecting it was an introduction to an important matter relating to Raya.

But the woman had fallen silent.

He nudged her with a question.

"I don't fully understand, Roseanna. What has Raya got to do with this story?"

"Your perception is sufficient, Mr. Radwan. Sheykh Tawfeeq is a kind man. Men like him make mistakes, just as all human beings do. He was obstinate and did not want to correct his error. But he regretted that later on, and he swore that he would let his second daughter, Raya, choose her husband freely, whatever his situation might be...."

"You mean...."

"I mean to say, your luck is heaven-sent. You've come at the right time. A thousand congratulations!"

Questions rose like waves in the sea, crowding his brain, competing with one another to get out. But Roseanna disappeared as though the earth had split open and swallowed her.

He called in a soft voice, "Roseanna? Roseanna? Where are you?"

She did not answer.

He knew that she could not have gone far. But she did not answer his call.

She had said what she wanted to and then she vanished.

Should he go back to his fiancée's house to ask who this Roseanna was? Was she the village witch?

Was she sane or was she a mad woman?

Who had put her across his path?

Like spearheads, the questions pierced his thoughts, but there was nobody to answer them. As darkness fell he decided not to return to Raya and began to review the dialogue in his mind. Before long, he began to feel more at ease.

Raya loved him, after all. She had not been forced to accept him. Her father had accepted him as a son-in-law because of his good qualities.

But who would assure him that Roseanna's story was true?

There were no answers, but he reasoned that the future would reveal many secrets.

He thought other people remained closed, isolated islands until you touched the edge of their shores, then the doors would open up and the secrets would become clear. You could then begin to enter the world of others just as you opened up your world to them. The two worlds would then blend, and marriage would take place, not just between a man and a woman, but between two worlds that were once apart.

He continued to ruminate. The howls of the jackals reached him from the vineyards and the fig orchards...Around him swarms of fireflies glittered, guiding him with their weak light. Near the horizon was the blurred figure of a woman wearing the night as a cloak.

50

Memories took him away from his present time and place. They carried him on warm, velvety arms like a mother's, and cast him into the lap of the secure past. He found rest and comfort in this lap. He did not resist, but enjoyed a pleasant sleep.

Days screened and winnowed out events. In the corners of memory, only the grains that filled the heart with joy and delight remained.

51

Radwan looked around him. Everything was the same as it had been before he had sunk into that pleasant sleep.

Um Nabeel was asleep, snoring lightly.

Simaan had had his fill of reading newspapers and magazines and was leaning against the window, half-way between sleep and wakefulness.

The other passengers were amusing themselves with conversation, drinking and smoking.

As for him, memories kept pulling at him secretly, diffusing their fragrance, spreading their beauty before his eyes, even stretching out fingers to close his eyes and bring him back.

"How many years have passed since those days, Radwan?" he asked himself.

Approximately half a century.

How was it that those events stayed so clear in his memory after all the other things he had experienced in his life had been forgotten?

Why was it that some memories did not vanish?

He snuggled down even farther in his seat, and with eyes closed went on another trip.

How often have I gone on a trip inside your eyes, Um Nabeel, he thought.

Her eyes were two thickets growing down the banks of the Hasbani River, floating serenely in its warm water, having stolen the color of the olives and the honeycombs of Jurat Al-Sindyan.

52

He definitely had to ask Raya about Roseanna the next time he saw her.

"Roseanna?" Raya asked in surprise.

"Where did you meet her?"

There were no secrets between him and Raya. He opened up his heart and told her everything the strange woman had told him. He carefully observed the reactions of his fiancee. Raya did not seem angry. She did not seem upset. But she made a comment, that day, which he would never forget.

"That crazy woman.... She sits at the entrance of the village like a witch, receiving those who arrive and bidding farewell to those who leave."

"Have I upset you, Raya?" he asked, his heart trembling lest he should have caused her any annoyance.

"Not at all," she answered. "You would have found out sooner or later. . .from me of course. We no longer discuss the subject when my father is around. He has lived in pain ever since he made that decision about Almas. His personality has completely changed. My mother and I are always worried about his health. My father used to be a merry person who loved people and the land. Now he has abandoned all that and he spends his time in silent, melancholy isolation. When he speaks to us, he speaks with a broken heart."

And thus, in brief, Raya brought him into the depths of her family life.

He thanked her.

From that day forward he made an effort to become close to her elderly father, often helping him in the vineyards and the orchards.

In one of those quiet times as they sat together, Sheykh Tawfeeq asked him, "Why don't you come and live with us, Radwan, my son? Our lands are in need of young arms like yours. As for me, my days are soon coming to an end."

Radwan was surprised at the request. In his mind, he had been building a little place in a garden where he would live with Raya, away from the interference of others. He did not know what to say. He heard himself muttering, "We'll see."

When he asked Raya for her opinion, her answer was simple. "We will live where you want to, not where my father wants."

And so he refused the generous offer, took his bride and moved into his dream nest.

53

How happy those days were!

His business thrived. Raya's face brought good fortune to his house — or rather, his hut.

The most important blessing was the birth of Nabeel, their first son. Now Raya would be called Um Nabeel, mother of Nabeel, as was the custom. Then came Lamya.

Um Raji, Raya's mother, attended each birth and stayed beside her daughter to the end of her confinement, and then returned home.

Raya's brothers were satisfied with her marriage to a young man she loved. They resumed correspondence with their parents, and good relations returned.

Yet all this did not change their father's condition. His worry grew larger and larger as the days went by. He became thin and gaunt, with the signs of old age clearly visible. Before long, he fell sick for several days and then he died.

After that, everything happened quickly.

Suddenly Radwan found himself in the midst of events, obligated to do so many things. He was the only man capable of managing the farmlands after Abu Raji's departure, as Raya's mother soon told him.

"No one is left to help us but you, Radwan," she said, hugging him, releasing her grief to him. "You and Raya must take the place of the absent young men. My son, leave the mill to your brother. Come and live here, in your house. The properties are in need of you."

Radwan preferred to live alone with Raya, even if it was only in a hut. But the woman was asking for his help — and he loved working the earth.

The job at the mill was only an occupation from which he gained his livelihood. As for the land, it was his passion and his heart's desire.

It was as if the woman's request was the earth calling for his strong arms.

54

Half a century of his life was planted in the soil of Jurat Al-Sindyan.

Under every grain of soil was a drop of his sweat and a ray of light from his eyes.

The crops of the farm were doubled.

He transformed the uncultivated fields into olive groves and apple orchards. He planted grape vines in the terraces of thorns and broom shrubs.

At gatherings, Um Raji spoke proudly of Radwan. "My good son-in-law has built up our place and made it flourish."

The hard work of his hands and the sweat of his brow gained him a new life and a distinguished position among the people of Jurat Al-Sindyan.

The reclamation of the land was not easy, especially when his properties were spread out in all directions around the village. He had to resort to using every bit of energy, experience and creativity he could muster.

During this time his family grew. Every year or two a new child was born until their number equaled the fingers on one of his hands.

Radwan swore that he would give his children a better life than the one he had known in his childhood. He sent them to school and created a comfortable life for them, away from the exhausting toil in the fields. When their primary education in the village ended, he sent them to Mr. Labeeb's school in Marji'yoon where they were able to complete high school.

And after that?

He choked as he remembered this period of his life.

It was not easy. He discovered that the learning they had acquired at school raised a wall between them and the land.

What was the use of a Baccalaureate diploma in an olive grove or a vineyard? What was the use of this diploma in the society of Jurat Al-Sindyan, which had remained the same for years and years?

He used to think that he had chosen the best way for them to return to the land, to the village, full of strength, experience, learning and self-confidence.

But "the account of the planting did not agree with the account of the harvest." It was not that simple.

For while he was planning for his children's future, their ambitions were traveling to places far beyond the boundaries of the village and its earth.

Nabeel was the first to broach the subject of emigration. Radwan tried to convince him to stay near and help him in the autumn of his life. But his words were in vain. Nabeel was determined to leave. Radwan felt that if he insisted, he would only create ill feelings in his son. And so he consented, after making Nabeel promise that his absence would not be longer than a few years.

Away from home in a foreign land, life was not easy, especially in the beginning. Radwan received letters that conveyed the most tender of emotions, the agony of an anguished and lonely heart, the traces of tears.

But conditions changed after Nabeel established a business of his own. He began asking for his brothers to come and help him or even continue their studies in Canada's schools.

Radwan felt utterly helpless.

He had nothing better to offer his children than work on the land. As he aged, his land became more and more stingy. The contagion of emigration spread among the young men. The village changed into a nursery that embraced the seedlings for a while, and when the trunk grew and the roots became stronger, the seedling would seek to be transplanted to a larger land.

55

Ten years after Nabeel's departure, the political climate began to change. The south of Lebanon became isolated from the other regions of the country; an official regulation required a transit permit for every citizen wishing to visit the south.

The people could not comprehend what was happening and how it would affect them.   In the depths of his heart, Radwan felt that the times were changing, not just because of his children's emigration, but also because of the blazing winds that began to blow from the south, carrying menacing threats, and later fire and destruction.

Villagers began to gather together. They authorized their mukhtars and mayors to meet the responsible persons in government. They sought explanations for the bad conditions and help for a situation that was beyond their control.

The delegations always returned, carrying empty promises.

And the days passed...

Time advances. It does not stop when faced by war or peace.

Radwan's own time also advanced, and his days became a life of constant waiting and expectation. Deep inside, he felt his waiting was in vain.

He waited for letters. He waited for his children to come home and spend the summer or to come home for good.

"O Father, in spite of great distances that separate us, we yearn for our home...."

"O Mother, longing burns our hearts. This alien land is not a mother's lap."

"O Father, the fire inside us will continue to burn. Its flame will only be extinguished by a drink of water from the village fountainhead."

He used to listen to the letters Um Nabeel read to him, and they both shed abundant tears.

They wept for life which was passing, and for the days which were going by. They wept for promises that evaporated in their hands.

It was no longer possible to make a single, sure resolution, especially after the war reached the south and the people began living between two fires: gun fire and airplane fire.

The fields lay fallow.

The trees withered.

The fires from the bombardment burned vast areas of the orchards along the Hasbani and in Jurat Al-Sindyan. The aggression continued. Time and again, the peaceful population paid the price. New victims were offered on the altar of war, and human justice was denied.

He no longer dared to ask Um Nabeel to write to the children as she had done in the past.

"We are waiting for you as though walking on glowing embers...."

"We will postpone the picking of grapes at the mountainpath vineyard until one of you comes home...."

"We are burning with desire to kiss our grandchildren...."

He stopped using these expressions in his letters, especially once all the people around him started convincing their children to emigrate to save them from death or an unknown future.

Deep inside Radwan felt what was happening around him was unnatural. And he remained incapable of understanding the international game that had chosen the south of Lebanon for an arena.

56

How would you describe your feelings, O Radwan?

What is happening around you?

Who are these human beings, sitting in their seats unconcerned, their eyes fixed on a silent silver screen where heroes are battling?

It is a movie, but your head is drooping, your eyes are closed, and you have not been following the events of the film.

You do not want to follow.

Your concern is to arrive safely at the next stop.

"How far have we gone, Simaan?" he asked. Simaan knew all the answers and had not surrendered to dreaming like he had. He answered Radwan quietly.

"Relief is in sight, Uncle Abu Nabeel. You were asleep and did not hear the announcement."

"And what did the announcer say, Simaan?"

"In a few minutes we will land at Montreal airport."

"Does that mean we've arrived?" He almost jumped out of his seat.

How did they surprise him thus?

How long had his absence been?

It had covered fifty years of his life. He jumped up from his seat and fell on Simaan, enthusiastically kissing his forehead.

"I can hardly believe it, Simaan! This means that we are on the other side of the ocean."

"Exactly," Simaan answered briefly.

He did not explain in detail as he usually did. It seemed that the kiss had surprised and embarrassed Simaan, especially when he saw the strangers nearby turn towards him, unable to understand the reason for this behavior.

Radwan returned to his seat.

"Prepare yourself, wife," he said jubilantly. "In a short while we'll land in Montreal. This means we are within two steps of the young ones."

He tried to sit but could not. He looked out the window, estimating the distance. His view was blocked by mountains of clouds.

He wanted to land the airplane, to guide it in with his eyes, to help the captain bring it down more quickly. He stretched out his hands as if to carry the jumbo jet.

His enthusiasm burned. It disturbed those around him. The hostess came and politely asked him to sit down and fasten his seatbelt.

He understood what she meant only from her gestures. He sat quietly, obeying her like a child. Joy shone in his eyes, and tears rolled down his cheeks.

57

Announcement followed announcement, in languages he did not understand. The plane changed its direction and his heart went with it. He reached out to hold Um Nabeel's hands, then he seemed to forget them in her lap.

58

He could not remember what happened in the next moments.

He was euphoric as though he had drunk two carafes of wine.

Without losing this feeling, he carried his small bag and walked behind Um Nabeel and Simaan, following the procession of strangers who had been his traveling companions.

They left the airplane-fortress as they had entered it, accompanied by smiles of farewell and thanks. They were met by vast halls — the halls of the Montreal airport.

Simaan's journey was to end here, and they would continue their trip to Halifax alone.

"I shall not leave you, Uncle Abu Nabeel, before I'm sure that you are on the airplane to Halifax. The monitor has just announced that your departure time will be in half an hour."

"Does that mean you will leave us here?"

Simaan had explained this clearly to Radwan before the flight but Radwan had forgotten. Could he be blamed for forgetting such a future detail?

But future details soon became present, urgent matters.

And here he was, surprised at this imminent separation from Simaan.

"God be with you, Son. May God make you prosper and succeed."

"What would have happened to us without you, my son Simaan?" Um Nabeel added. "Go with God's blessing."

59

Simaan waited until the plane was ready to leave, then entrusted his two traveling companions to the hostess. He asked her to take good care of them, especially since they did not know the language. She stayed with them from then on. She walked beside Um Nabeel, and gave her a helping hand when she noticed her difficulty in keeping pace with them or in climbing the stairs. She did not leave them all through the one-hour flight from Montreal to Halifax.

"Good people are everywhere, Um Nabeel," Radwan said. "Without them the world would be ruined."

"May God never deprive us of good people," Um Nabeel answered.

"She reminds me of Lamya," Radwan continued. "Don't you see some resemblance?"

"That's what you think, husband! Nobody in the world resembles Lamya!"

Her Lamya.

With large, honey-hued eyes, chestnut-colored hair, white complexion, high cheekbones and a charming smile.

Lamya!

Where could one ever find anyone who resembled her?

Abu Nabeel was simply passing the time talking, she thought. That's all right. She had no objection to that.

In her heart, she felt as anxious as he was to reach their destination. But ever since she married him she was accustomed to suppressing her feelings and keeping her thoughts and opinions to herself, lest he disagree with her or she should hear an unpleasant word that would upset her.

He became accustomed to her submission and silence.

She took in everything but would not show emotion, even in moments of intimacy. Not even once did she permit herself to express a sigh or a sound.

He would pose a question, and she would answer without hesitation, "As you wish, husband."

He would consult her on a matter and she would respond simply, "You're the one who decides."

That was how she lived with him, peacefully, quietly and happily.

But was she happy?

She had never asked herself this question. The opportunity had never presented itself.

Why would she ask when she knew her role. She performed it with love, as a wife and a mother.

Sacrifice and self-denial: paving the paths of her loved ones with the soft light of her eyes and all the love in her heart so that they might grow in light, joy and hope.

Here he was beside her, as he had been for half a century, holding her hand in moments of pain, distress and anguish. He led her through life, as he had led her in that distant moment still recorded in her consciousness when he answered the priest, "Yes, I take Raya, daughter of Tawfeeq Abu Nijim, as my wife...."

60

He helped her to take her seat and then sat beside her. He automatically fastened his seatbelt.

Simaan was not here for him to consult, and he would not bother the hostess. He now knew what was required. When there was an announcement from an invisible place in the front of the plane, he understood what they wanted. He extinguished his cigarette, leaned back in his seat and took a deep breath.

Like him, Um Nabeel prepared herself and sat attentively, full of expectation. In a short while they would meet the young ones.

"What do you think, wife? Is Charl'ton far from the airport?"

"My guess is as good as yours, husband."

"They certainly will come to meet us at the airport," he assured her. "They certainly will."

61

The plane took off, spurred on by his expectations and eagerness. The hands of his wristwatch moved much too slowly. They turned as if they had to go all the way around the globe.

He himself had been spinning around the globe since that morning.

If only he had known that he'd already crossed a distance almost half the distance around the earth. The sun accompanied him and refused to set before safely placing him in the lap of the young ones.

This observation had not escaped him. He turned to Um Nabeel to share his thoughts with her.

"Have you noticed, wife, how long this day has been?"

"The sun has accompanied us for twenty hours," she answered. "Our day has been nearly two."

"That was lucky!...not to take this trip at nighttime, I mean." He added these last words for her sake.

Night and day were all one to him. Could travel in this giant fortress be more difficult than his night trips between Jurat Al-Sindyan and the neighboring villages? Riding his donkey, traversing the mountain paths and desolate wastelands with the howl of wolves and other beasts of the wilderness?

How could it be compared with his hunting trips for porcupine and grouse on pitch-black nights?

The hostess left him no opportunity to continue his conversation or to daydream. The announcement came over the loudspeaker that usually preceded the shaking of the plane before landing.

62

He expected to see them standing in the open space of the airport waiting for him, their eyes searching and their faces overflowing with joy.

He leapt from his seat and hurried off the plane with the agility of a twenty-year-old.

"Wait for me, husband," Um Nabeel called out. "Where are you going?"

"To look for the young ones."

The hostess was close behind him but was unable to catchup. She was saying something but he could not understand her words.

"The young ones are waiting behind the glass window," he said. "Don't you see them gathered together there?"

He forgot the hostess and Um Nabeel in his rush to look behind the glass.

They were strangers...

They were all strangers. No face was shining for him, and no eyes opened like the gates of Paradise.

Where were they? They had to be somewhere.

The hostess gave up. She held Um Nabeel's hand and led her to a seat in the waiting room. Then she left to attend to her other duties.

Radwan continued to fidget restlessly like a nestling bird that had fallen from its nest and couldn't find its way back. After half an hour of exhausting search in front of the glass windows, he returned, short-tempered and impatient, to Um Nabeel.

"They did it. They did it to us, wife... May God curse life in strange lands."

"Be patient, husband," she said, trying to calm him down. "Be patient. The young ones will not abandon us. Certainly there must be some misunderstanding."

"Misunderstanding?" he retorted angrily. "There certainly is misunderstanding between us and all these creatures. Look around you. Are you able to give and take with a single one of these people? What will we do now?"

He spat out his words. They stung her as though they poured from the crater of a volcano.

Feeling at her wits' end, she did not know how to answer him. She would have lost her temper had she not seen a hand waving to her behind the glass...

63

The hand of mercy was being extended to Radwan and his wife, here in this cold airport which greeted them with indifference. Someone was waving at them!

Um Nabeel looked intently at the woman's face and tried to remember who it could be, but it was in vain. Despair seized her again.

"Perhaps the woman is mistaken. What shall we do, husband?"

Radwan scrutinized the face of the woman carefully, observing the direction of her eyes, then turned around to look to see if she was looking at anyone else.

There was no one there but them.

Finally he said, "I'll respond to her, come what may."

Um Nabeel agreed and kept her eyes on him as he slowly went towards the closed window.

The woman signaled to him, pointing to the exit.

She repeated his name and smiled kindly and tenderly.

This woman could not be a stranger!

He returned her smile and nodded to show that he understood. He returned to where his wife was sitting and asked her to come with him.

64

Moments later they were face to face with the woman. She embraced Um Nabeel and kissed her warmly, welcoming her in Arabic. She then put her arms around Radwan and hugged him.

He watched what was happening like a lost person.

In her enthusiasm she had forgotten to tell them who she was.

She apologized. "I'm sorry. I must introduce myself...I'm Jane, Jane Habeeb."

"You mean you're the sister of our son-in-law, Fayez?"

"Exactly, Uncle Abu Nabeel. The young ones asked me to meet you and take care of you. I live here in Halifax."

"Where are the young ones, ma'am?" Radwan was still disturbed and anxious; he did not understand what was happening.

She smiled.

"The young ones," she explained, "are half an hour from here by plane. In a moment you will fly to Charlottetown. They will be at the airport to meet you."

65

So that's what it was. The whole thing was a misunderstanding. Perhaps it was over-enthusiasm on his part. He had not listened well and had not asked for more information. He had not paused to think of distances and stops.

Half an hour's distance by plane! Of course he did not expect the young ones to make such a trip to meet him here!

Matters became clear. His anxiety subsided and Um Nabeel's face brightened up with a smile.

"We'll go in this direction," Jane said. "I'll take you to the plane and wish you a happy ending to your journey."

He took in each of her words eagerly, wondering, "Will it really be the end of the journey?"

In the last hours since Simaan had left him, distances seemed longer. He began to think his journey would never end.

66

The fourth airplane of their journey was waiting for them.

It was small in size, an old make, humble, simple.

Radwan felt its friendly atmosphere as he squeezed himself into the narrow seat with Um Nabeel crowded in beside him. They were both reminded of the first bus that had traveled the newly paved road of Jurat Al-Sindyan.

"It's only half an hour, wife, and we'll be there."

He retained his joy and enthusiasm. Indeed, his excitement was at its height when the plane flew quite low, allowing him to watch the sea and the land, a land he never dreamed of reaching.

"This is Prince Edward Island," the hostess said. He understood her announcement because he had heard this name so many times. He was there.

To him, the Island meant Charlottetown—it meant arriving.

The flight left him no opportunity for reflection: the plane landed like an eagle descending from high mountain peaks. And like a partridge, it began to move swiftly along the runway.

It carried him close to a small building that was painted green and grey.

"This is Charl'ton airport, Um Nabeel."

And here they had gathered together as he expected and dreamed in his waking hours and in his sleep.

Nabeel was in front. Near him was his wife, Salma, and their children. His brothers and sisters with their families surrounded him. In another circle relatives were gathered: cousins from both sides of the family. Finally, there were friends, his people from Jurat Al-Sindyan whose emigration to this province had begun ninety years earlier.

67

In the moments that ensued, Radwan and his wife were like a ball being tossed from hand to hand...like a musical instrument on which many tunes were being played.

They surrendered to hugs and kisses, to tears and smiles, to words mumbled in confusion in order to fill the awe of the occasion, the silence that reigned, reminding the witnesses that this was a turning point, a decisive moment in life, a milestone in history.

Radwan did not sober up from the intoxication of the reunion. He did not turn around to see individuals from other groups standing close to the walls, their eyes wide open, as if asking themselves what on earth was going on here. They did not understand and nobody thought to explain it.

Had Radwan not been so involved in the reunion, he would have turned to them as he had turned to the stone buildings of Jurat Al-Sindyan. And as he had spoken to the pigeons above the red-tile roofs in Hasbaya, he would have said, "We're paying a visit to the young ones, my friends, a six-month visit. And then we will return home."

68

His heart was full of pride and elation. Here he was with his family. He was so proud of them.

His children were all successful. He had not come to reassure himself of their success. He had believed every word, every story that was reported to him. But what the senses could record was so different from those lifeless words that had come through the mail.

Nabeel opened the door of his home for them.

He asked his mother to stick a piece of leavened dough on the lintel above the threshold.

Um Nabeel refused.

"This is what the bride does, my son. And your wife has already stuck such leavened dough there years ago, and its blessing is with you wherever you go."

But Nabeel insisted. "I want you to bless our home with your holy hand, Mother, the hand that nourished us and accompanied our step with blessings and abundance."

Um Nabeel gave in, for any request from her son was dear to her. She took the leavened dough and with her five fingers pressed it above the door. Applause and good wishes rose all around her.

69

A generous table full of blessings was prepared for the arrival of the dear guests, most important of which was the arak, a drink which carried the aroma of the vineyards of Lebanon. Then there was the food which also kept the flavor of the motherland.

Once again, Nabeel took the initiative in the conversation. He asked his father to say grace and to take the first sip of *arak*. He then followed suit, raising his glass and proposing a toast.

"To your safe arrival."

Then he invited everybody to sit at the table.

Radwan had been wandering about in his world of dreams for the past seventy years.

Occasionally the dreams were nightmares.

In good times, he lived in the most wonderful moments of ecstasy.

And here he was returning to a blissful dream which had abandoned him in recent years since the menace to his precious land began.

He did not believe that he could now be awake.

He was merely going back to one of his past happy dreams.

But how could a dream fill his heart with this overwhelming joy. How could it so delight the soul, rise to his head, then turn and turn, meanwhile recording the laughter in their eyes, the happiness, the chirping of the little children, and this blend of young voices.

These voices mixed the language he understood with another he did not, leaving gaps between the expressions. These gaps were dense when he turned his ear to the little ones who gathered around him...the fruit of twenty years of love!

These were his grandchildren.

Could this be true?

They kissed him on his wrinkled face.

They kissed his rough, lean hands.

They let him hug them, and hold them between his arms and feel their breath on his forehead and the warmth of their bodies which spread to his own and planted new energy there. This new strength moved him and filled him with joy and happiness, making him feel that he was obtaining his due in life. This great reward was coming all at once, as when good fortune is handed out in abundance without warning.

"To your health, Father."

He heard their toast.

"Praise be to God for your safe arrival."

Meanwhile, Um Nabeel digested her joy silently, contemplating the loved ones around her, and quietly drying her tears.

What words could describe her feelings? What words could express the emotions surging in her heart?

Arms encircled her, sometimes embracing her neck and sometimes her shoulders. The precious faces descended on her like flights of hungry birds, pecking kisses from her rosy cheeks, reminding her of the seasons of drought she had lived through since the emigration began. At the same time they reminded her that these moments would not last. For she was here for a few weeks or a few months, and then she would return home.

She contemplated her husband.

She tried to read his expressions, and noted he was in a state of joy that had taken him far away from her, as if he were preparing to fly.

And, lo, here he was, jumping off his chair, leaving the dining table, surprising everyone.

She saw him snatch a pink shawl from the shoulders of Lamya, their daughter. He knotted it around his waist and hips and began to dance.

She knew he had reached that point where she could never follow. He began to turn and go around the table, around his children and grandchildren and around the invited friends, leaping gracefully and nimbly as though he were a partridge.

The scene aroused a wave of enthusiasm and applause which made Nabeel get down the *dirbakka* hand drum from one of the shelves and start keeping time to the beat of his father's dance. This brought them all back to their first home in Jurat Al-Sindyan and to the days when Radwan was in the prime of his youth. This was the special language he used to express his feelings, the language of his body merging with the group through melody and rhythm, through distant memories that overwhelmed him.

This is the way the azarole tree
Is stripped of its leaves and fruit, Mommy.
This is the way the coquette walks
And acts, Mommy: this is the way.

His aging body moved like a palm tree laden with fruit, blown by stormy winds that made it sway but not bend.

His hands moved, stripping an azarole tree as they had done for thirty, forty, fifty years.

His joy spread over his wrinkled face, it radiated from his eyes and overflowed with every movement. All eyes were focused on his body, seeing but not believing.

How was their father, their grandfather, able to preserve that nimbleness and grace?

If he were to stop for a moment and ask himself, he would have posed the very same question. How was he able to preserve his favorite language which brought friends and companions around him on evenings of pleasant entertainment, for village weddings, when the stamp of his foot reached deep into the ground, connecting him with the furthest point the roots had reached?

The circle expanded.

The young men and women rose, the warmth of his body filtered into theirs, invisibly connecting them with him, irrespective of years and distance.

The warmth touched their bodies, awakened them and intertwined them in the circle of the age-old Lebanese *dabka* dance.

His daughter Nawal turned on the cassette player which began playing popular and favorite songs by Fayruz, Wadee', Sabah and Nasri.

Yet the dabka dance was not complete until Jibran, Nabeel's friend, left then returned after a few minutes.

Jibran had emigrated ten years before Nabeel.

70

Jibran Abu Hamad.

Jurat Al-Sindyan had known him in his adolescence, and in the prime of his youth. He was tall like a poplar tree, handsome like a prince, merry like a songbird chirping in the vineyards.

And like a songbird proud of its voice, he used to strut around the streets of the village singing ballads and playing his flute.

He had come to the reception for Radwan but had not brought the flute. And when the dabka circle had formed to the tunes of the recorded music, his old enthusiasm returned. So he left the circle for a few minutes, and came back with his flute. He stood in the middle of the circle playing the time-honored tunes, stirring up the passion for dancing in everyone's hearts.

71

When Radwan became tired of the dancing, he sat down near his wife, contemplating the waves of joy flowing in the house of his eldest, joyfully sipping every drop of pleasure and feeling that what was going on around him was beyond reality.

Drinks, food, music, dancing, and then Jibran and his flute.

Was it possible that Jurat Al-Sindyan would be transported with all its people, customs and traditions to this faraway and very strange island?

Yes, they have been transported.

The people he knew half a century ago had emigrated, one after another. Jibran had been here for thirty years and had not forgotten the music. He sought the magic of the old melodies that could erase the emptiness and sadness that clung to his soul.

Jibran, who was a prince among the young men of Jurat Al-Sindyan, was brought to this island by a woman.

72

The world was just coming out of the Second World War which had spared no corner of the earth.

Among other places, it had hit Jurat Al-Sindyan.

The young men were the most affected, for the doors to earning a living were blocked. Dry seasons seared the earth and the harvest was poor. The old men remembered the specter of the First World War and their hearts ached.

When the truce was declared, the villagers welcomed a tide of expatriates who returned to check on their relatives.

Marina Fayyad was among them.

Rumor had it that Marina had come to look for a bride-groom worthy of her and her wealth.

Radwan did not believe the story and considered it merely one of those rumors which the cunning men of the village spread in order to entertain themselves.

The truth was soon told when Marina led Jibran into the "golden cage" of wedlock.

He was twenty and she was over forty, well-preserved under layers of flesh. People thought Jibran had made the worst deal in his life.

The woman lured him not by her beauty or wealth, but by her passport.

Marriage opened a wide door for the young man to escape his poverty and travel beyond his narrow horizons.

73

And here he was, thirty years later, playing the double-reed flute. Five years after he arrived, the arguments started and Jibran and Marina were divorced. Radwan did not known all the details of the story, but he observed its traces written on Jibran's face, expressed in the dull light of his eyes, his bent back and the painful anguishwhich rose up with his melodies. They kindled nostalgic feelings in the listeners' hearts and awakened sleeping memories.

But the time was not for memories and regrets. Jibran could not be as miserable as he appeared. He now owned a clothing factory. As for Marina, she lived in Ottawa.

What happened to Marina?

Perhaps the question would be answered later on when Radwan could fully enter this new society which perplexed and troubled him. It had turned his mind into a broadcasting station that transmitted questions and answers with lightning speed, never allowing him to reach a state of tranquillity.

He used the occasion to open his suitcases. He took out the gifts and distributed them. Hands seized them anxiously as if they were receiving blessings that had come from Holy Heaven.

When he was reassured that everyone had received his or her gift, and nothing but that little bundle remained in the suitcase, he was filled with confusion. Should he take it out and convey Roseanna's message or should he leave it for a better occasion?

"But this is the best occasion, Radwan," his inner voice whispered as if prompted by Roseanna's spirit.

Radwan was encouraged and took out the bundle. He paused, as though he was preparing himself for a speech.

"One moment, friends. May I have your attention, please?"

He then turned to his children. "It was Roseanna who made me carry this gift to you. You remember Roseanna, the one and only. I was about to lock my suitcase when she stopped me with this package in her hand. Do you know what she said?"

Radwan did not receive any response, nor was he expecting one.

"She said, 'Abu Nabeel, I trust you to take this gift to the young ones.' In it is a handful of soil, which Roseanna gathered from the vineyard overlooking the valley. 'Take it to the young ones, Abu Nabeel... The young ones must miss the scent of the soil of Jurat Al-Sindyan.' This is what Roseanna sent you. I used to think she was crazy. But her words took me back to my deepest roots."

Silence reigned. Hands sought handkerchiefs to dry warm tears.

A handful of soil!

Nabeel took it from his father and said, "We will put it in a crystal vase and place it in the most honored part of the house. It will be an object to cherish, a shrine for all of us."

74

What could he say after that?

Radwan felt completely empty as if he had shot all the arrows in his quiver: words and gifts, as well as joy and dance.

He finished his message and sat down.

The light in his eyes dimmed.

The guests began to say good-bye and leave.

The party ended.

It was past midnight and the two travelers were exhausted.

Salma, Nabeel's wife, showed them to the room she had prepared. They followed her silently and listened quietly to her instructions about opening the doors and closets, how to turn on the water faucets, and lastly, how to use the television set.

Radwan, who was an expert in the use of machines known in Jurat Al-Sindyan, found he was completely ignorant regarding the use of even the simplest machine in his son's house. Even the opening and the closing of a door here required a special lesson!

This world was strange and extraordinary.

He remembered that he had started his trip against the tide of his years, against the flow of his days. Ever since he had set foot on the threshold of the Canadian Consulate in Beirut...

This was to be the greatest adventure of his life.

His own past had not been boring by any means. But it was within his grasp—he could understand it and control it. Even surprises were not surprising on the banks of the Hasbani River and in Jurat Al-Sindyan.

Here, however, everything seemed strange. Even friends, children of the same village differed from what they used to be and from the image he had painted in his mind.

With these thoughts he fell into a deep sleep.

When he awakened, the sun was not there to receive him. He opened the curtains and looked out the window. What he saw filled him with wonder and surprise. The clouds veiled the space in front of him and hung so low that they touched the treetops in the garden.

The trees were succumbing to the early autumn storms that stripped them of their beautiful rainbow-colored leaves.

There were birds, which seemed to fear neither rain nor storms, jumping from branch to branch. Some were large, much like grouse. Others were like sparrows but brilliantly colored. These birds lived among people, unafraid of hunters' bullets. They came near houses with the daring of the first creatures in history.

The hunting instinct moved in his breast, especially when he saw flocks coming from every direction to join the others, then flying confidently into the air screaming fearlessly.

He tried to remember the last time he had seen birds flying above the trees of his village or its vineyards, but he could not. He then thought that their disappearance was related to the constant air raids that bombed Jurat Al-Sindyan and the southern villages.

Generation after generation, people of his village had watched the birds of September pass overhead in a single line, at the same time of the month, year after year. Even those birds had disappeared in recent years and left many questions behind.

Some of his friends suggested that the birds had changed their route. Others joked that the birds decided not to migrate, preferring the cold of the North Pole to the gunfire and bombs.

And there were others who thought that some seasonal birds had tasted death before reaching the boundaries of his village. They had been annihilated by the chemicals that the peasants sprayed in northern countries.

There were many theories. He did not know what to believe.

But he knew that a change had definitely taken place and the beautiful birds had disappeared: the bee-eaters whose shrieks announced the end of summer, the pelicans with elegant legs, the sparrow hawks, the grouse, the quail...and all the other meek birds which created a warm atmosphere by their passage, that filled the void left by the young ones in the season of migration. For the young ones used to leave the village about that time of year after being brought together by the summer season. Then they would leave the village, returning to school, to jobs or to distant lands.

75

He stepped back from the window and went to wake Um Nabeel so that she might enjoy this rare morning scene with him. But she was sound asleep.

He let her sleep. He tiptoed to the door and opened it. He heard whispers coming from below, specifically from the kitchen.

He closed the door quietly and went downstairs...

76

Radwan followed the voices, his nostrils filled with the aroma of coffee and cardamom. His children were doing their best to cloak their strange environment with things familiar to him, such as last night's banquet and this morning's gathering. Here they were all waiting for him, sitting around the kitchen table: Hassan next to his wife Ra'ida, Jameel and his wife Ferial, Nawal and her husband Fayez, and Lamya and her husband Mu'een. Nabeel was making coffee while Salma prepared pastries for their breakfast.

And the little ones?

"Where are the children, Nabeel?"

"At school, Father."

That was right, at school. Today was not a holiday. The young men and women had not gone to work so they could be with him and Um Nabeel. They all got up, one by one, to embrace him with a warmth that made his tears flow.

Nabeel's kiss was accompanied by the coffee pot and the little cup he knew his father liked.

"We don't want anything to be out of the ordinary for you, Father."

"May God keep you and protect you, my dear ones."

One blessing followed another as he saw them moving around or heard them speaking. He invoked God for their prosperity and long life; he invoked Him for their success, safety and happiness as well as for their children and their spouses. All he could give them was his blessings and his benediction. And he gave these generously, his eyes running over with satisfaction, engulfing them all.

"Did you say the children were at school, Nabeel?"

"Yes, Father. Our schools open at the beginning of September."

"God bless them and grant them success." The grandchildren were in need of his repeated blessings. There were now sixteen and others were "on the way." He loved little ones, especially if they were his own descendants — the promise for immortalizing his name in future generations. This was his greatest ambition: to live on in the children.

77

"Thank God, wife, they're like the children of kings."

That's what he said later in confidence to Um Nabeel as he sat with her, sipping coffee and enjoying the warmth of these happy moments together.

"They're the spitting image of their grandfather in beauty and charm," she teased.

He responded immediately.

"Beauty, they took from you. From their grandfather, they took only cleverness. What do you think?"

"True, true. I don't disagree with you. Thank God for this blessing."

A moment of silence passed between the couple, like a pause for rest. Then Radwan said, "Do you know what I'm thinking, Um Nabeel?"

"How can I guess, husband?" she answered. "Your ideas are always ahead of mine."

"I'm thinking of our grandchildren's future. Do you think they'll ever come to Jurat Al-Sindyan?"

The question awakened her as if from a deep sleep.

"What makes you think of these things now? We've only just got here."

"I must think, wife. In fact, the idea has never left me. It has been boiling in my heart ever since our children left. Will they ever return? And if our children themselves find it difficult to return, how much more difficult will it be for our grandchildren...who were born here, who grew up drinking foreign milk and speaking a foreign language? Didn't you notice them yesterday, trying to talk to us in their strange language and how, when we spoke to them in Arabic, they smiled but were unable to answer?"

Attempting to change the subject, she said, "This is a matter for later on. Why do you heap worries on your head? Rejoice in them, now. Whatever God sends us, I say, how sweet it is!"

"On the contrary, Um Nabeel. We have to think of this matter and discuss it with our children. I'll speak to Nabeel about this, at the first opportunity."

78

The conversation worried Um Nabeel.

She was on a short visit and had made a pledge to herself not to interfere with the affairs of the young ones. What was the matter with her husband, muddying clear waters and creating problems?

But she felt more at ease with the idea when her husband mentioned their son Nabeel. For she knew her firstborn well enough, and she knew that he could handle any problem with calm thinking and wisdom, without angering or upsetting others.

79

A week after his parents arrived, Nabeel returned home from work one evening to be greeted by his father. Radwan asked if they could find a quiet corner for conversation.

"There's an important matter, Son, which I would like to discuss with you."

Nabeel was taken aback by his father's serious tone and he prepared himself for the situation.

"Go ahead, Father. I'm at your command."

"Why, my son, do your children and the children of your brothers and sisters not speak the language of the homeland...our language?"

So that was what had been troubling his father. He had noticed signs of concern on his father's face since he had arrived. He was doing his best to make things easy for his parents and to offer them everything that would make them comfortable and happy. In spite of that, there had been a cloud hanging in front of his father's eyes.

Nabeel had thought that being in a foreign land was the cause.

Everything here was new to his parents. Undoubtedly, they must have noticed the changes that each member of the family, as well as the friends, had undergone. The image in their mind painted from the past was being shaken and replaced by another. This was natural. He had expected it. As for the subject of language, he had discussed it several times with his brothers and sisters, but the daily routine of work and conditions of their environment continuously overwhelmed them and swept away all decisions.

In the previous year, he and other immigrants had decided to open a private school where their children could learn the Arabic language. But it was difficult to find a teacher and the children themselves lacked the desire, for they had no strong motive to sacrifice the time reserved for play and favorite hobbies in order to learn a language not even required in their school programs.

His father's question awakened all these ideas. After some thought, he answered, "You're right, Father. We have been negligent here. We are remiss. We come home exhausted at the end of the day and we need rest. The children live in their own world. Society and school take them away from us....The more they grow up, the more independent they become."

"And does this make your children happy, Son?"

Again his father was posing a basic question that awakened his consciousness to the fact that he was leading a monotonous, mechanical life, overwhelmed by his work.

But he could not help answering, "The children entertain themselves with hobbies: music, sports, trips, and then there are their friends."

"Do you think, Nabeel, my son, that this is sufficient? Don't they need to know something about their relatives, their forefathers, their roots? I'm not trying to interfere with your private affairs, but we do have a duty to our children...."

Radwan trailed off.

He felt he was digging deep into the past and dusting off memories. He too had many duties towards his children. What did he give them? What did he offer them but a desolate land and unemployment? And here they were in an alien country because of his own failure.

He thought of this and looked into the nervously blinking eyes of his son Nabeel, recognizing his anxiety and the turmoil in his soul.

He knew this habit of Nabeel's. Since childhood, his eyes had revealed feelings that were stirred up inside and he could conceal nothing.

He was anguished to know that he was causing Nabeel pain—this noble-hearted person who had stretched out his hand to his brothers and sisters. He had pulled them out of a life of poverty and an uncertain future to give them a renewed life, an opportunity to work and live in this new world so full of promise.

He put his hand on Nabeel's arm.

"Don't be concerned with what I've just told you. That was only emotion stirring in my heart, excessive enthusiasm on the part of your father, who is attached to his ancient world to the point of obsession."

Nabeel smiled at him.

"Don't regret what you said, Father. Your words have touched the heart of the matter. But one is unable to have everything one longs for."

80

But the subject was not closed.

Nabeel brought it up again one evening when his brothers and sisters were all gathered together, without their children.

"Our father has raised an important subject," he began, "namely, that our children don't know our language. This is something that we're all aware of, and we feel it is creating a chasm between our generation and theirs. What can we do about it?"

Nawal was quick to respond. "The subject is being discussed among all immigrants, Nabeel. It has also been brought up at the university. Our children are facing a problem which is more important than just language—"

"What do you mean, Nawal?" interrupted Nabeel.

"The problem of belonging," she answered. "We're the first generation who immigrated to this country and they are the second, the one born here. Do you see what I'm getting at? They know that we don't belong to this society, to its traditions and customs, to its way of life or to its language. Even if we speak the same language as Canadians, our accent is different. In spite of all that, we're a part of Canadian society — in our daily affairs, in our work, as well as in the education system. When we come home from work, we return to the private environment we've created. It is not the environment of the village back in the old country, nor is it the Canadian environment. It's a mixture which has grown between two worlds, between the two societies."

"But this doesn't bother us," Hassan interrupted. "On the contrary, we are proud of our origins, of our traditions."

"Sorry, Hassan," Nawal rejoined. "Perhaps I've not made myself clear.... The matter is different as far as our children are concerned. They don't know any world other than this one, and they haven't lived in any environment but this one. It is only natural that they adopt the clothes of the people of this land, follow their example in life style, in customs, as well as in language."

"Our children are not one hundred percent Canadian, Nawal," Jameel said. "They still keep many of our traditions and ways."

"Okay, I agree, Jameel," she answered. "We did give our children a great many of our good traditions and customs that we're proud of. But this turns against them sometimes."

"Nawal is right," Lamya agreed. "We've all heard our children complain about being teased by their classmates when they speak the occasional word of Arabic."

"This is a natural reaction among children," explained Nawal. "They don't like our children when they hear them speak another language. Naturally doubt would arise in their minds. They feel that the conversation is about them, that our children have banded against them. That's why they react this way."

Salma added, "That's also why our children ask us not to speak Arabic around their non-Arab friends. Nawal, you remember the day Rudy came home from school after a fight with his classmates."

"But is it necessary for us to give in to their complaints and do what they want without discussion?" Nabeel asked.

"The problem, Nabeel, my darling," Nawal said, "is not that of our children alone. It is the problem of the second generation of immigrants in general. As I already said, it is not a language problem so much as it is a social problem, a problem of belonging. The

Arabic language has not yet become a mark of distinction. It is still the language of an immigrant group that has come to this country in search of livelihood."

"Will there come a day when Arabic becomes a mark of distinction?" Jameel asked.

"That depends on future developments," Nawal answered. "And it's related to the status of the Arab immigrants. I notice good signs on the horizon. For a while, immigration was restricted to the uneducated class; today we find university professors, doctors, lawyers and other educated young men and women among the new Arab immigrants. These people create a positive image of our homeland. As a consequence, the old image of the ignorant immigrant carrying a peddler's pack on his back is being changed. Right?"

Hassan suddenly became defensive. "Not right at all, Professor Nawal! This immigrant who carried a peddler's pack on his back is the one who opened up difficult roads by his hard work, his sweat and his ambition — despite his ignorance! This immigrant has a right to be honored by us, by Canada and by other countries open to immigration. He contributed greatly to their growth and development, and played an important role in establishing the cornerstone of their society!"

Nawal answered quietly, "Sorry, Hassan. I didn't mean to belittle the importance of pioneers. All I'm trying to do is to shed light on the current situation which neither you nor anybody else can ignore."

81

Radwan listened to his children's discussion apprehensively. He was afraid it would lead to disharmony.

He almost regretted having brought up the subject in the first place. He pondered what Nawal had said about the new image of the Lebanese expatriate who now had university degrees in place of a peddler's pack. The image of the young men lined up at the airline office and at the Beirut airport jumped into his mind. They had bright faces, coming to a new land, but what a void they had left behind!

82

His country was, and continued to be, a generous nursery in which the seeds grew. As soon as they flourished, the hands of successive generations and unseen wills uprooted them. They were then transplanted to lands beyond the horizon, beyond the seven seas, at a distance far beyond imagination.

Images of successive waves of emigrants still lived in his mind from the days of his early childhood. Their faces were dim, like embers covered by the ashes of passing years. Then came this invitation leading him here. Homesickness flared up in his heart like fire in dry straw, and memories came back, tumbling before his eyes.

83

Why was he here?

What was the reason for coming to this land of cold and alienation?

Of course, to visit the young ones; to get acquainted with his grandchildren who were born in this foreign land and were growing up in it; to carry back home with him their warmth, recharged by it in the winter of his life, sustaining him in his days ahead. Days ahead?

What would his days ahead bring?

He could hardly answer this question.

He had come here only a few days ago. He was only here for a visit and he never thought of opening one of those doors that led to the future.

Here he was sitting in a corner he chose at his son's home, by a window that overlooked a wide street. He was smoking, meditating and talking to himself.

You've changed a lot, man! Since you first stepped on this foreign soil, you've gone far away from yourself. Immigration has become a wall separating you from your roots. Long have you dreamed of seeing their beloved faces. Often you have prayed that God might realize your wish and return them to you. This is how you always used to pray. You asked that they return. You never thought that you'd ever go to them yourself, accompanied by Um Nabeel, by your seventy years, by the mass of grey hair on your head, and by your ignorance.

Yes, this is what eats you up: your ignorance.

This distance between you and them, twenty years too long, is a barren, flat desert in which you have not written a single word to sustain the relationship. Every day the winds of alienation have passed over, drifting layer after layer, leaving this distance open, remote from your protection.

This is the crux of the problem.

Now you've come to them carrying your heart in your hands, eagerness in your eyes, and these dormant hopes and dreams. You've tried to come close to them, one step at a time. But you feel that they are going away from you, slipping between your fingers like quicksilver.

Why are they moving away from you in this way?

They're your flesh and blood. They're the sap of your life and love. What secret element entered their blood and caused them to go so far from you? Yet is it really they who are going away or are you the one unable to catch up? And, so, your imagination is creating delusions for you.

Don't you remember how well they all received you and your wife? Don't you remember the warmth of their faces, the welcoming emotions they spread out like a red carpet for you to step on? Don't you remember the love and the good intentions? All they wanted was your satisfaction. What's the matter with you, man?

His thoughts wandered.

It is they who have changed. But this is the way life is. We change every day. You've changed. The people who emigrated from your village, Jurat Al-Sindyan, and whom you've met one by one since your arrival...they've also changed.

It is difficult for you to tear up their old pictures in the pocket nearest your heart, and exchange them for new ones.

Perhaps this is the reason, for you did not expect to see them thus.

It is difficult to wash away the traces of half a century in the wink of an eye.

It was necessary for you to face them as they are, but you failed to see the painter who, pail and brush in hand, worked every moment of the day and night, diligently and persistently changing everything.

Haven't you seen Jibran's face and how it has changed?

And Najwa, too. The apple of Jurat Al-Sindyan, the blooming rose who left the homeland a few years before Nabeel, carrying in her pocket the picture of an unknown young man who had asked her hand in marriage.

Where is your bridegroom, Najwa? Or are these the traces that remain of him, wrinkles around a tightly closed mouth, dejected eyes, and an aging body?

How about Saleem, your neighbor's handsome son? On the day Saleem left, you embraced him as you would one of your own children and you brushed away the tears that flowed from his blue eyes, eyes that were the color of the Beirut sea at its clearest. What happened to those translucent blue eyes? Will the clouds of the Island forever hang in front of them or will the sun rise again in your eyes, Saleem?

And Shaheen, your cousin, the "tiger of the wilderness." How could expatriation tame you, Shaheen? How could it rob you of your health? How could it transform your tiger's legs into two weak sticks riddled with arthritis?

And Nabeeha, the lily of Mount Hermon. Oh Nabeeha! You used to say in your secret moments of great joy, Radwan, "Nobody rivals Um Nabeel's beauty except Nabeeha." Her eyes were the narcissus of the valley, her hair the fine fibers of the night spun over the pine forests, her complexion the snow of Mount Hermon when the spring sun shines on it!

Nabeeha tied her destiny to that of the wealthy immigrant, Badee' al-Mu'izz, and their wedding was the joy of the village. You yourself danced until sunrise and Jurat Al-Sindyan celebrated the event for ten nights, thanks to the generosity of the bridegroom. The photograph of the "lily" in her flowing gown next to the starched stiffness of the bridegroom still decorates the place of honor in your home and in the homes of relatives. On that day, Badee' gave pictures of his wedding with the candy boxes to all the relatives so that it would stay deep in their memories—and on the walls of their homes.

Nabeeha received you with tears and apologized for Badee's absence. "He's become a cripple," she said. "I've been taking care of him for twenty years."

Then she added, drying her tears, "My eyes have not been dry since I left Jurat Al-Sindyan."

You tried to ask, "What about your children, Nabeeha? Don't they make up for the great difference between you two?"

And Nabeeha shook her head, saying, "Don't you believe it, Abu Nabeel. Children of this country belong to this country. Don't listen to anybody who tells you otherwise."

"Why don't you return to Jurat Al-Sindyan, Nabeeha?"

Your question silenced her. She did not answer. And you asked yourself, if Nabeeha returned to Jurat Al-Sindyan, would the narcissus return to her eyes?

Yes, man. This is the real situation which has touched you so deeply and stood as a wall between you and the people here.

Nabeeha taught you that first lesson in what final immigration meant. She opened your eyes to the future. She told you that Canada's children belong to Canada. That is, they are no longer your children and your grandchildren. They will never return, no matter what their birth certificates say. Words written on paper are nothing but words.

The truth is in this sea, surging with the winds of change...And you paint this dark picture in your eyes as though inspired by the clouds hanging over this Island and surrounding the roofs and forests. You forget, man, forget that the transformation they have all undergone has been the price paid for success that goes far beyond the confines of the mind.

Najwa has accepted her fate and dedicated herself to the education of her children. She gave the three of them to Canada. They are well-educated university graduates who have good jobs.

Jibran has no children but he has established a very successful factory which is the envy of everyone.

Saleem, whose highest ambition in Jurat Al-Sindyan was to take care of his land, now owns a big clothing store.

Shaheen would have remained "the tiger of the wilderness" had Canada not tamed him and given him the opportunity to become the owner of the biggest hotel on the Island.

As for Nabeeha, she compensated for her husband by having successful children. They've told you of her eldest son who is a lawyer and one of the assistants to the prime minister, while her daughter is a famous movie star. If Nabeeha would look at the bright side of her life, the sun's rays would dry her tears for the rest of her life.

The important thing is how you yourself judge the situation, Radwan.

Each window in this room has a different scene. Similarly, the faces of people differ. Yet you insist on standing in one fixed place, dragging your children into taking a stand with you. They must repeat your words, learn your philosophy, and accept your insistence that there is no happiness outside that small spot of land called

Jurat Al-Sindyan. If this were true, how, pray tell, do the rest of the people live?

84

Radwan woke up from the strangest dialogue he had ever had with himself, and felt that he was returning from a dream that had snatched him out of time and place, carried him far away then dropped him in a jungle of questions before bringing him back to reality.

He turned around, but saw no one. He did not hear even his wife's voice. He was lost and lonely.

Um Nabeel! Where was Um Nabeel?

85

"Do you like Canada, Michael?"

The little one did not answer. Um Nabeel sat with her three-year-old grandson on her lap, playing with him and teaching him children's games, using her hands and all kinds of gestures to communicate with him. "Stretch out your hand, grandson. Stretch it out like this. God bless you!"

The little boy understood and imitated her as he sat in her lap silently. He instinctively felt that this lap was his throne and that he had the right to enjoy it in peace and tranquillity. He followed his grandmother's frail fingers, copied her movements, then looked up at her face as if to ask, "Did I do it right?"

She took his palm in her hand then, holding each of his fingers in turn and said, "Here is a water pond. A bird came to drink. This finger caught it, this one slew it, this one plucked out its feathers, this one roasted it, and this one let it fly away... Tweet, tweet. . .fly away...birdie, bird!"

The little one laughed with all his heart. He did not understand the story but he gathered from the gestures that it was a funny one. He stretched out his hand again. His grandmother held it tenderly, raised it to her lips, kissing it.

"May your hand be ever safe and sound, my love."

He pulled away his hand. That was not what he wanted. He motioned to his grandmother to keep playing.

She remembered another game and took his soft hand between hers. "This is the palm for the gold dinar. This is the wrist for the bracelet. This is the elbow for the basket. And this is the hole of the mouse...kur, kur, kur!"

She tickled the child's armpit and he laughed, spreading joy through her heart and in the quiet, still air. She did not let the occasion pass without stealing a kiss. She felt that she was getting her reward of happiness.

If only they would leave him to her all the time.

If only!

She remembered his elder brother and sisters, as well as his cousins. She could easily make herself understood by the little ones. As for the older ones, she did not know how to approach them or how to speak to them. She felt cornered, unable to reach into their world. She remained in her corner, watching them play, read or laugh as they filled the air with their noise and strange conversation. She would remain in her corner while they grew without her presence, as they had done when they were only an image in her mind and a name on her lips, from news in their letters, voices recorded on tapes. She thought in those distant days that meeting them would remove all ambiguity and mystery. Then, she would speak to them face to face, in her own tongue, and they would understand every word of hers... Were they not her blood and her soul? Were they not arrows shot out beyond vision, beyond the reach of her heart?

And here was one of them filling her lap with warmth and happiness, and her mind with anxiety and helplessness.

She remembered her husband who was in the next room. She admitted to herself that Abu Nabeel was right: mutual understanding would not be easy between them and the grandchildren. Misunderstanding would always continue as long as this alien language was the bridge that could connect or separate the generations.

Then there were other matters besides language, such as social behavior.

She had begun to notice the freedom the children had, without fear of being scolded or restrained by their parents. They acted in a natural and spontaneous way. They were boisterous, they quarreled, they did whatever they liked: no father or mother stopped them.

That was not how she had brought up her children. And even if she was tolerant, she knew Abu Nabeel did not approve of this kind of behavior. Deep inside, she wished he had the will to restrain himself and not interfere in a matter which did not concern him.

Besides, what did she or her husband know about this new world where their children and grandchildren lived? Maybe this was required behavior: unlimited exuberance without control or restriction.

It never occurred to her to compare her old way of life with this one to see which was better, for she was not ready to embark on a journey through an endless maze..

.She was preoccupied by these thoughts when Abu Nabeel entered suddenly, muttering her name.

"I'd lost you, wife...where have you been?"

"I've been with Michael," she said merrily. "I was teaching him some games."

She motioned to Michael to go to his grandfather. But the little one ignored her.

There had been a dialogue between them and he found comfort in playing with her. He was not ready to take one step towards the old man standing in front of him.

When the grandmother insisted, the little one escaped from her lap and went to his playroom.

She was left alone with her husband. A thought came back to her. "Why have you raised the subject of language, Abu Nabeel? I'm afraid the young ones will be upset. We're just here on a visit, is that not so, husband?"

"Perhaps you're right, wife," he said resignedly. "Yet it is so difficult for me to see that I can't communicate with my grandchildren...my own flesh and blood. I speak to them, but they stand silently in front of me, like statues. With them, I'm like a deaf man in a crowd. What do you think of all this?"

"I'm in no better situation than you," she said quietly. "The difference between us is that you want to reform the world, whereas I accept things as they are."

Radwan nodded. "That's true...I hope you'll remain as you are, Um Nabeel. Believe me when I say I've raised the subject in spite of myself. I've not come here to disturb the young ones, but this is our opportunity to learn how they live. Did you understand what Nawal said?"

"I understand Nawal even when she does not speak. Of course, her words were philosophical but they were clear."

Radwan seized the opportunity to express his admiration for Nawal. "Praise be to Him who created her! Even the deaf would enjoy listening to her. For a long time I had thought she would excel at learning. And here she is, shining like a star. But. . ."

"But what? You always open closed doors."

"No, Um Nabeel. My hesitation is out of concern for my children. She was speaking and I was listening to her proudly, thinking at the same time that every word she said increased the distance between her and Jurat Al-Sindyan, though I wished that everyone there could hear her."

"Will Jurat Al-Sindyan be the criterion by which you measure everything forever?" she said excitedly. "The important thing is that the children succeed and live happily, wherever they are!"

"That may be all right for you, wife! God has granted you the blessing of accepting reality, but He has afflicted my heart with constant anxiety."

Radwan then came closer and surprised her with a tender embrace.

"What would have happened to me if I did not have you, Um Nabeel," he muttered.

Her shyness made her blush. She instinctively turned around to make sure no one was spying on them. She heard her grandson singing in the next room.

Reassured, she let her husband's arms encircle her. She put her head on his shoulder and felt her heart pounding strongly, as it did on the day they first met.

87

Radwan and his wife were almost alone in the house.

The adults had gone to work, the children to school. Michael, who was too young for school, was staying with them.

Visitors came to see them less often now. After the welcoming rituals were over, their attentions had returned to their jobs.

Radwan began to think of the future, and the coming days seemed long and monotonous. He felt surrounded by an invisible ring that imprisoned him in two kinds of alienation: one of expatriation and the other of language.

Nobody here knocked at his door.

Nobody here called out to him, "Anybody home?" so that he might answer from inside the house, "Come in, please come in."

Any time of the day or night his porch received guests—lifetime friends, hunting companions, people of all ages.

His was an "open house." That was the expression the citizens of Jurat Al-Sindyan used when speaking of his humble little home on the hillside overlooking the village. His door was never closed to anyone who knocked. It was even without a lock until the day he left Jurat Al-Sindyan. Then Farhan, the tinsmith, came and put one on.

He used to consider the lock a personal insult to his very being.

Why should he lock his door?

To keep out whom?

Thieves ?

What thief dared to come within one step of his fence? Furthermore, where would thieves come from? The people of Jurat Al-Sindyan lived together as relatives and in brotherly love. How would thieves go among them unnoticed?

Here, however, he was a prisoner. Even the weather robbed him of his freedom, of walking in the streets, of being apart of nature.

It was the end of September, the month of harvest and fruit-picking in his country, while here the temperature had gone down close to zero. The sky was overcast with clouds and did not promise sunshine. The winds carried threats of the coming storms. If this was the weather in September, what should he expect come December and January?

He stood wondering in front of the window, his eyes roaming freely over unfamiliar scenes until they reached the far horizon without hitting a hill or a mountain.

The Island was flat like the palm of a hand. It had neither hills nor valleys. Nabeel had promised to take him on a fishing trip before everything froze and the fish left for deeper water. Then he would see more of the Island.

But now all promises seemed put off until later. He moved from room to room, from window to door, catching glimpses of the neighbors' houses.

Neighbors? With all these lawns and gardens separating them?

No. There were no neighbors here. Even if there were neighbors, they were strangers. He did not dare to open the door and step out.

Even the street here spoke a language he did not understand.

What were all those signs? How far did all these broad, flat lines of roadways stretch? Where did they lead?

He asked those questions but did not search for answers. He knew one thing for sure: if he tried to walk along one of those lines, he would end up in frustration, with an even greater sense of alienation. He should therefore stay at home, enjoy the warmth and the comforting companionship of his wife and little grandson. He remembered an old proverb, "A woman gives you warmth in the winter of your life." This proverb applied to him now as he approached winter unprepared.

88

Returning from his meditations, he took the transistor radio in his hands. It resembled the one that Nabeel had sent him a few years back. It had been his constant companion, connecting him with the world and all the new things in it.

He turned it on and began to move the dial, looking for any one station that would greet him. From right to left, the dial moved. He stopped when he heard music or announcers' voices, only to find his isolation further emphasized by the tongues of these strangers. He moved the dial to another station, then realized that all voices here resembled one another and that the music was all the same.

Suddenly he was surprised to hear a tune that revived old memories, reminding him of songs he had grown up with and was greatly fond of. But he had left them behind, there among the vineyards of Jurat Al-Sindyan, on the banks of the Hasbani River, among the haughty poplars, the shy willows, the arrogant sycamores and the proud oleanders. There in the seasons of gathering grapes, stripping olives and harvesting wheat, the warm and tender tunes rose to fill the air and transform the quiet into festivals of joy and serenity. There one's mind was set to rest, one's soul humbly resigned as though in the final sleep.

But the tune was deceiving, for it soon revealed its true nature and was no longer familiar to Radwan, leaving him to his scattered memories. He filled his empty moments by comparing all that he saw and heard and felt here, with what he had left behind before embarking on this trip of a lifetime.

Um Nabeel observed him silently. She felt he was anxious and bored, and she knew the radio was adding to his frustration. Wishing she could somehow help him, her eyes moved to the telephone.

"Let's call Lamya and ask her when she's coming to see us," she suggested. "Yesterday she promised she would come over."

He looked at the telephone nervously. "You call her," Radwan said.

He was not trying to avoid speaking with Lamya, but he was afraid of this strange instrument which resembled a serpent, the head of which was in one's hand with the tail connected to the unknown.

His anxiety increased when his wife said, "I don't remember the number."

"And who said I remember it?" he retorted irritably. "The young ones should be calling us."

In his heart he was thinking that being stung by a serpent might be easier than the shock of a strange voice if he dialed the wrong number.

Um Nabeel called to her grandson in another attempt to bring some joy to Radwan's soul. "Come, Michael. Come, dear."

The little one responded quickly. She motioned for him to turn on the television. Strange and wondrous worlds began to open up on the screen as if part of a magic city was transported into the room.

The attempt succeeded. Radwan sat down comfortably and began watching the actors' movements, trying to guess what was going on by following the gestures and the tone of voice. Michael sat beside him, his eyes fixed on the moving pictures. He would shout or laugh or jump to his feet. The grandfather could not help showing how delighted he was with his intelligence and wit.

"Michael understands better than we do, wife. What do you think? Are we going to remain this way, like a deaf man in a crowd?"

She answered without turning from the screen. "In order to understand this country, we should become like children."

"Become like children," Radwan joked. "You alone become one, honorable Um Nabeel. I've made up my mind to return to the homeland at the same age as when I left it, neither older nor younger!"

Um Nabeel laughed at her husband's words, and they both echoed their grandson's laughter which had reached its peak with the program he was watching.

Suddenly, a harsh ringing silenced their laughter and their conversation.

Radwan did not know whether this meant he had to open the door or answer the telephone, but he felt a force stronger than his will pushing him toward the door.

89

Radwan's intuition was not wrong. The ringing was from the doorbell. When he opened it, he saw Shihadeh al-Asmar standing there, wearing an overcoat and a fur hat with flaps covering his ears.

"Shihadeh al-Asmar! My God, how small this world is! Who ever thought we would meet here, Shihadeh?"

Taken by surprise, Radwan embraced his old friend. With his arm around the man they went inside.

"Um Nabeel," he called out to his wife excitedly. "Come see who is here!"

Eagerly his wife got up to receive the guest.

"Welcome, Shihadeh, welcome. How have you been? How is our sister Fareedeh?"

"Fareedeh is fine, and sends you greetings. She could not leave the store and come with me. I hope we'll be able to come together next time."

Um Nabeel did not seek further explanation. She knew that Fareedeh worked outside the home like many other women. But she listened to Shihadeh explain in detail.

"Fareedeh has taken care of the store since we arrived from the old country. She learned the language and was able to communicate with the customers. As for yours truly, I've remained useless and harmless like a young donkey."

"What are you saying?" Um Nabeel interrupted. "You're a highly respected person, brother Shihadeh!"

The guest sat between the couple as though on a throne. Even if an angel had descended from Heaven, he would not have gotten as warm a welcome as Shihadeh received from his two friends, especially at this hour of the day. He had saved them from boredom, and brought them joy and liveliness.

He continued the conversation as if he had come to fill them in on everything they had not yet learned since their arrival.

"This country, here, belongs to the aggressive and the clever," he said. "He who does not work does not survive."

Radwan agreed. "That's true, Shihadeh. This is a country of hard work and constant motion. He who does not work dies of boredom."

"You've said it, Abu Nabeel. You can't find a single person here to visit with or talk to when you feel like it. Frankly speaking, if it were not for your young ones, I would have lost my mind long ago. Your children are the reason for us living here. Otherwise, my wife and I wouldn't have known where to settle."

"Life is difficult," Um Nabeel added, "both in the homeland and in this land of emigration. The world has changed."

Shihadeh agreed. "Indeed, the world has changed. That is a fundamental truth. Do you remember the good old days, Abu Nabeel?"

Radwan listened to his friend. He had been waiting for him to bring up this subject. He begged Shihadeh's permission to leave for a moment to fetch the coffee pot from the stove. Then they resumed the story, a story rooted in half a century of their lifetime.

90

This was Shihadeh. After a twenty-five-year separation, Radwan was seeing his friend again.

He poured the coffee and offered the first cup to his guest. He gave him a cigarette, lit one for himself then sat down comfortably.

"Your winter starts early, brother Shihadeh."

His friend smiled as he returned to a far-off place, to a country of constant warmth and sunshine. That place had brought them together in the prime of their youth, then cast them to the winds of time.

Their land was an expanse stretching from the foot of Mount Hermon to the farthest point of Mount 'Amel. In that stretch of land they experienced youth and early manhood. Shihadeh al-Asmar hailed from Dair Mimas, a calm village of olive trees on the southern border of Lebanon. Shihadeh owned olive groves and wheat fields. He was a young man who worked the earth, communicating with it in all languages and seasons. Between one season and the next, there was always time to enjoy certain hobbies, especially his favorites, hunting partridge and fishing.

How did he get to know Radwan...

Radwan looked keenly into his eyes now, trying to connect with what had been cut off during their long separation. There, in that country whose walls were painted with friendship and warmth, where a human being did not grow like a lone tree but was one of the forest. In a corner of that world so far away from them, they had come to know one another at the mill. Then Radwan was a miller of uncertain future. Shihadeh used to load sacks of wheat on the back of a strong mule, then set out towards the "walnut mill," called so because of the tall walnut tree that spread its shade and fragrance over the mill and its waterwheels.

In that atmosphere overflowing with freedom, tranquillity, flour dust and the dreams of youth, Shihadeh used to spend many hours after his wheat was ground helping Radwan. They talked and dreamed of the future, while discreetly following the women with their eyes.

On other days, Shihadeh used to come to Radwan on his mule, with neither wheat nor bulghur. He used to wait until his friend finished working, then they went together to fish in the streams that flowed sleepily under the shade of the oleanders and willows.

When they could go for longer periods, they used to take trips to the foot of Mount Hermon or the hills of al-'Urqoob where the partridges liked to fly, heedless of hunters.

91

Those days were long gone. There came the day when they parted, as the patterns of work and married life separated them. Then Shihadeh emigrated.

"I did not believe it, Radwan, when Nabeel told me you were both coming to visit Canada. I wanted to come to the airport to meet you, but I had a bad cold and had to stay in bed. The weather here does not help—fog, cold and dampness."

"I've noticed it," Radwan said. "Since our arrival, the sun has not shone once."

Shihadeh nodded. "This is still summer, so to speak. There are worse days to come."

This was not news to Radwan, for he had learned it in his children's letters—their descriptions of the severe climate in this area of Canada so close to the North Pole.

He used to hear news of Canada's weather and record it in his consciousness without exactly understanding its meaning. Then he arrived here and began to experience the weather first hand.

Shihadeh continued. "In the old country they used to say, 'Between October and November is a second summer.' Here, even our summer is winter."

Suddenly Shihadeh fell silent. He felt he had gone too far in speaking about the harsh weather. He realized he might make the new guests despair, so he added, "However, the houses here are equipped with the most modern heating systems... No air or cold can seep into the buildings."

"But one is deprived of walking in the street," Radwan said.

His friend agreed. "That's true. But one can get used to anything."

92

It was true, one gets accustomed. Radwan did not object to this idea, for his children had become used to living in this difficult climate. His grandchildren were like "fish in the water." And here, too, was Shihadeh in front of him. He wondered whether Shihadeh had grown accustomed to Canada's climate and whether he, too, had become like a fish in the water.

He posed a question, to test him. "Don't you ever think of returning to the homeland, Shihadeh?"

His friend took a deep breath before answering. "I've returned five times, so far. On each trip I took my wife with me and I said to myself, 'Man, there is no place for you as good as your homeland and your village. I have no children and I don't wish to die in an alien land and be buried under the snow.' But..."

"But what, Shihadeh?" Radwan asked anxiously.

"Let me confess to you and my sister, Um Nabeel, about my true feelings. Every time I went to the homeland, I felt I was getting farther away from it. The homeland is no longer what it used to be. Dair Mimas has changed. People our age have departed this life or have moved away. On our last trip, we could not even reach our village—road blocks, weapons, and the smell of war and fire were everywhere. As soon as I set foot in Beirut, I decided to return here."

"What do you intend to do now?" Um Nabeel asked. The conversation had aroused an unusual curiosity in her.

"Sister Um Nabeel, our work here is fine. Fareedeh and I have become accustomed to the climate. It's true that I have not learned one Canadian word but my wife helps me. And the children of our homeland are here and they are loving, especially Nabeel and his brothers and sisters, may God bless them. They make me feel like I'm among relatives and members of my tribe. Recently we began to hear the news of war. They said, 'War in Lebanon is inevitable.' Is this true?"

The question took Radwan back in time, and he tried to gather images that had fled from his memory since he had set foot in this neutral and peaceful country. He remembered the news of the first two rounds of war, the tense atmosphere when he went to Beirut, the long lines of young men trying to leave the country, the continuous threats on the southern borders. He remembered and wondered, could this have been the big war?

He turned to Shihadeh.

"Brother Shihadeh, our homeland is indeed not at rest. There are developments which do not bode well. People in our region no longer remember how the good old days were."

"I don't read newspapers and I don't understand what the radio says," Shihadeh said. "However, friends here speak of nothing but the forthcoming war, and they say that they read this in the newspapers."

"May God bring what is good." This was Radwan's usual invocation when he had nothing to say or to add.

Shihadeh then threw in an unexpected question. "Have you come as immigrants to stay with the young ones, I hope?"

The question stung Radwan like a branding iron and he rose to defend himself and the true purpose of his visit.

"No, Shihadeh, no. The purpose of our trip is to visit the young ones, and for six months only. Then we'll return."

"Six months? That's a short visit! You should stay for at least a year!"

But then he added thoughtfully, "I have a feeling that the young ones will not let you return, especially in these conditions."

His friend's words broke down the thin wall standing between Radwan and the future. For the first time he began to see an aspect of the truth he feared and escaped from every time someone discussed the future.

He tried to convince himself that Shihadeh's words expressed a personal opinion unrelated to what his children intended for him. Even if they thought of keeping him in Canada with Um Nabeel, he would refuse to comply. He would absolutely never accept, even if this might anger them. He would never permit anybody to chain him, to limit his freedom and make him live against his will in a particular place, even if that place was the Garden of Eden. He then felt he was committing a sin letting his thoughts run before him thus. He returned to the present and to his natural decisiveness.

"The time has not yet come to discuss this matter and the young ones have not broached the subject."

"Their aim is to win you over and keep you with us as long as possible," Shihadeh said. "At any rate, time will tell."

Um Nabeel broke in, "May God set our minds at peace so that we may all return to the homeland... An alien land will always remain alien."

93

Radwan eyed his longtime friend, trying to read in his face thoughts other than those expressed on his lips.

And this is what he read: the face was pale and wrinkled. It had long ago lost the fingerprints of the sun and the southern winds. The hair was gone from his head except for fringes around the edges. The eyes were clouded and Radwan did not understand why they reminded him of the eyes of fish — you looked intently into them but could not penetrate their meaning.

On the lips he read silence and an interrupted dialogue, especially that dialogue which arises between man and humanity, between man and the earth — nature, people, soil, trees, birds...

A humorous thought occurred to Radwan and out of the blue he asked, "Tell me, Shihadeh, do the birds here speak Arabic?"

Shihadeh laughed. Radwan's question was a good joke. "It never occurred to me to listen to them, Radwan. Perhaps the birds here speak English!"

"You mean to say they wouldn't understand our partridges and turtledoves?"

Radwan's statement took Shihadeh back to his old passion for the chase. "Here we hunt wild geese during hunting season, and of course the geese speak in sign language," he laughed. "As for your son, Nabeel, he hunts deer."

"How about fishing?" Radwan asked.

"On this too, Nabeel, the chief of all fishermen, knows best. We are all soldiers under his command. Nabeel knows all the rivers and streams. At times, I think there must be a wireless contact between the fish and him. For as soon as the fish open their eyes after the numbing winter temperatures, they send him their first telegram."

Everybody laughed.

"You exaggerate Nabeel's feats!" Radwan said.

Shihadeh answered, "Experience is the best proof. Accompany Nabeel on one of his hunting or fishing trips and you'll see it's the truth. But don't you go without me!"

94

This, then, was Shihadeh al-Asmar.

He was still the same as when he had left the homeland a quarter-century ago.

Canada had not changed him a bit. It did not add a word to his language or an accent to his speech. His conversation still flowed with its original innocence as though it had just come out from beneath the olive trees of Dair Mimas.

Why did Shihadeh emigrate and drag Fareedeh along with him?

How could emigration benefit a person after his roots had hardened and sunk deeply into the earth of his country? When he came to uproot them, would they not rebel and resist, leaving him to carry his head in his hands, lost in a daze?

Why did he emigrate when he was doing so well there, living comfortably with no children to worry about and thus free from any future commitments?

Radwan would have asked his guest these questions, had he not noticed these dark looks that Shihadeh cast as though he was trying to say something more but restrained himself.

95

He was in this state of silent dialogue when the door opened without warning. It was Lamya, holding the hand of her youngest daughter, Suzy.

"Good morning, Mother. Good morning, Father," she said joyfully. "Welcome, Uncle Shihadeh."

She turned to her daughter. "Say 'Good morning, Grandma. Good morning, Grandpa.' Come on, Suzy...'good morning.'"

Suzy put her finger in her mouth, hesitated and leaned against her mother's leg, turning her head away and shrugging her shoulders.

Lamya protested. "She is shy, but it doesn't take very long for her to get used to people. She just needs time."

"Of course she needs time," Radwan said. "How could she ever know that this old man is her grandfather and this old lady her grandmother? Hey, Suzy, apple of your grandfather s eye! How could you possibly know us, since you were born here and have always lived here?"

When the little one heard him speak her name, she became even more bashful and clung harder to her mother. Lamya pushed her gently away as she said, "Let's go. I've come to take you out for a drive. Uncle Shihadeh, you're welcome to come with us."

Shihadeh thanked her. "Uncle Shihadeh will return home. Thank you very much, Lamya. I must go. Good-bye."

He wrapped his head warmly, put on his overcoat and started to leave. But Lamya stopped him. "We'll take you home with us — it's on our way, Uncle Shihadeh. It's too cold outside."

96

It was cold like most of the months were here on the Island. One had to prepare for the weather, adapt to it and accept it as people in this country had done. They harnessed nature, they tamed it, they controlled it with the power of the machine. Man here rose and stood tall, higher than trees, higher than the tops of the mountains. Man in this country was a giant and the results of his progress were evident everywhere.

Radwan went down the stairs that led to the garage where Lamya's car was parked. The car was warm and had comfortable seats. It was like sinking in a pile of ostrich feathers.

Lamya started the car and drove down the street confidently. Radwan sat in the back seat, contemplating her. His eyes never had their fill of her.

This beautiful woman returned him to his youth and reminded him of her mother at that age. The beautiful eyes were the same, the high cheekbones, the stately dignity of her neck, the goodness of her heart. If only he could stay here forever to enjoy the warmth of her youth — that would compensate for the cold! But these thoughts would pass as the evening breeze over the leaves of the poplar trees, touching his feelings, dancing with them for a moment, then abandoning them and disappearing. Nothing would remain but memories.

He knew well that this sensation would leave as soon as his heart stirred with yearning for the homeland. For faces and voices, for familiar scenes in that secure corner where he could walk with closed eyes, and yet clearly see everything around him, hear and understand all that happened — from a single hint or tone of voice.

Here they were, transporting him in a car, traveling on this wide road that reached to the edges of the horizon. His daughter was a skillful driver. Yet he was afraid of surprises, of the unknown. His eyes were wide open so as to take in everything. But the images would soon die out like lights in a city preparing to sleep. His eyes would not remember a single scene to carry back home. The scenes of this country would remain for the people of this country, like everything else.

The car passed through the streets of Charlottetown, the quiet and simple city that did not resemble Beirut in the least.

His eyes journeyed through the window to the changing scene as though looking at pictures in a peep show box: wide streets, clear sidewalks, colorful houses situated amid gardens and forests. At times he thought the houses were planted in these level lands, just like trees and people.

"Where is everyone, Lamya?" he wondered.

"Your question is a good one, Father," she said. "The people are at work inside the buildings, and the students are at school. The cold weather here chases people from the streets."

"There aren't many people here, anyway," interrupted Shihadeh. "Only the hardiest immigrants are able to reach this Island."

Lamya explained further. "Uncle Shihadeh is right to a certain extent, for this was the case for the immigrants long ago. Nowadays the Island prospers because of man's ability to conquer the harshness of nature. It's a great challenge to man's capabilities and energy. And man has been responding. The result is this progress and growth.

"Naturally," she added wryly, "the density of population becomes less as one moves farther to the north."

"Brother Radwan, you could say we are on the boundary of permanent ice and the land of human beings," Shihadeh joked.

Radwan commented, "In spite of that, it's quite prosperous and inhabited. Amazing! God bless the hands that build!"

97

Deep inside he was saying something else which he did not want to express to anyone. He was asking Shihadeh, Lamya, and the young ones now absent, how in the world they had come to this cold country and how could they tolerate living in it, season after season, year after year.

Questions like those he knew would remain unasked until he could understand everything around him and become part of the daily life.

Had his friend Shihadeh, after twenty years of living here, arrived at this kind of understanding?

But there was no time for an answer.

The car stopped suddenly in front of a small building. Shihadeh got out and thanked Lamya. He invited them to come in for a cup of coffee. He pushed the door open and shouted, "Fareedeh, Fareedeh come quickly!"

Fareedeh hurried down the stairs and over to the car.

"Welcome, welcome," she greeted them. "You must honor us and come in. You can't just pass by. Our home is yours."

Lamya apologize for everyone and promised them a visit in the near future. They drove away, Shihadeh and Fareedeh waving from the front of the store until the car disappeared from sight.

"We'll pass by Nabeel's store first, then we'll go to Hassan's restaurant," Lamya said.

"Are we having lunch at the restaurant?" her mother asked.

"No," Lamya answered. "We'll have coffee at Hassan's after we see Nabeel's store. Then we'll go to my house. I've prepared a delicious meal for you. Mu'een will be waiting for us."

"As you wish, my love," Radwan said. "We're in your hands."

"Rather, you're in charge, Father. Everything we own is yours."

Nabeel owned a supermarket in the center of the city. When they arrived, he was waiting at the entrance, with a smile of satisfaction radiating from his eyes.

"Welcome. A thousand times welcome."

He held his mother's hand and led her in. Lamya, Radwan and Suzy followed.

The store was crowded with customers and overflowed with all kinds of different merchandise.

"May God pour down His blessings and grant you success!"

Radwan walked around with Nabeel who explained to him everything that was unfamiliar. Um Nabeel sat on a chair and waited because her legs hurt and she could not walk for very long periods. Her eyes traveled for her, following every movement. She prayed in her heart that God might guard the store and its owner. Um Nabeel feared the envious, evil eye that could split rocks with its malicious power. She had memorized a special prayer against that eye. Who deserved this prayer more than her firstborn who built his success with the strength of his own two hands and with drops of his blood.

"It's his sweat and his strong right arm. My dear son!"

When she received his money orders, she'd raise them to her lips and pray for his further success. Now, she was sitting at the very fountainhead from which abundance had flowed for twenty years.

"May God bless you, Nabeel. You take a handful of soil and it turns into gold, my son!"

Now here he was, approaching her, his father beside him with a joyful face opening like a flower on a spring morning.

"What a wonderful store this is, Um Nabeel! May God's name bless and preserve it! It is He who grants success and prosperity."

Um Nabeel answered, "He has been blessed by the Lord and he deserves these gifts. May God continue this blessing and bounty to you, your home, and all that belongs to you, Nabeel."

Her son thanked her. "All this is because of your benedictions, and in answer to your prayers for me and my brothers and sisters. May God not deprive us of your parental blessing."

"God will give you even more blessings," Lamya teased, "if you would listen to me and come and have lunch with us!"

Nabeel considered her invitation. "Impossible, Lamya. I can't leave. This is the busiest time of day. Go now and have lunch. Tonight, we'll meet at my home and have supper together. So, until later...."

He accompanied his dearest guests to the car, then returned to attend to his customers.

Lamya then drove to Hassan's restaurant, "The Town and Country." Hassan had called it thus so that he would not forget his roots sunk in the depths of Mount Lebanon.

100

Hassan was very emotional and much like his father in his anxieties about the future of mankind. Like him, he was also interested in the arts and had a beautiful voice that was as moving as that of Wadee' al-Safi, the famous Lebanese singer.

He was sitting behind the cash register when the door opened and a group entered that looked different from his usual customers, be they workers or members of parliament.

He jumped to his feet. "Welcome! A hundred times welcome!"

"Welcome to you, Son," Radwan said. "What a wonderful restaurant, Hassan! It really warms my heart."

"Do you like it, Father?"

"Do I like it? What a question! Thank God you and Nabeel are successful. Soon we'll see Jameel's beauty parlor as well."

"You should take Um Nabeel to have her hair done," Hassan teased. "That is the only way they'd let you in a beauty parlor!"

Radwan knew Hassan was joking and this revived his old weakness for this son who was so strong, energetic and good-hearted.

They are *all* good and have hearts of gold! He rebuked himself for these thoughts that destroyed his parental impartiality. He knew he should not favor one over the other. How could he do that anyway, when he always considered them as one person whenever he thought of them?

Hassan asked one of the waitresses to set a table for his parents. Lamya objected and tried to convince him to come to lunch at her house. But she did not insist, knowing how difficult it was for her brother to leave during the lunch hour. So she apologized to Hassan, took her daughter by the hand and led her parents out.

"Mu'een is at home by now. We're late for his lunch time. He usually eats early."

"We'll tell him it was our fault," her father told her. "We'll stick up for you and save you from blame."

He then smiled, assuring her that he was only joking to make her feel better.

101

Mu'een set the table and brought the drinks. The food was in the oven, waiting for Lamya's hands to serve it.

"I haven't cooked a fancy meal," she said. "It's only broiled fish, *taratur* sauce and parsley, grilled *kibbi* and lettuce-and-tomato salad."

"All this food, and yet you apologize?" Um Nabeel asked.

"It's most delicious," her father praised her. "God bless your skillful hands!"

Lamya smiled as she went between the kitchen and the dining room. "You know the old proverb that says, 'Hunger is the best cook.'"

Mu'een asked her what the proverb meant.

"You should ask your father," she answered. "He is the best person to explain proverbs."

Mu'een suddenly jumped up. "Lamya," he said, "I've forgotten to bring my father! The poor man has been waiting for me for half an hour! Please excuse me for a few minutes!"

102

Ibrahim Waked was the first Lebanese immigrant to set foot on the Island. That was in 1888 — the date had been recorded in the family book. However, he was not the first of the pioneering Lebanese emigrants. Before him, in 1882, had come Ibrahim Abu Nader, a nineteen-year-old man from Zahleh, who had settled in Montreal.

Ibrahim Waked came from Rashayya al-Wadi, where he had left behind a wife and two children to wait for his safe return. But he did not return. Ten years later, in simple Arabic he wrote the following letter to his wife:

From Canada, March 17, W.

Dear daughter of our uncle,

From a far distance, and out of insurmountable longing, I kiss your cheeks eagerly, and send you abundant greetings of peace. I hope to God that you are well. On our side, we are fine, thanks to the Lord's providence. All we lack is seeing you, may our Lord grant that — for He is capable of anything. I am writing to inform you that we have sent you a letter and with it a money order in the amount of thirty English pounds. I hope to God it reached you. We asked you to inform us how much debt you owe, how much in pawns, and to whom. Inform us in detail, and we are ready, with God's help, to pay back all those who lent you money and we pledge never to forget their favors.

Our aim is that you should come to join us here. We will send you all necessary papers and expenses. Tell us about people in the village, from beginning to end, who has died, who is still alive, because we want to know. The date of the money order is February 17, Western calendar. My work is very good, my health is fine. Remain at rest with

regard to us. Give our greetings of peace to all who
ask about us. We kiss your cheeks. Keep well.

Your uncle's son
longing to see you,
Ibrahim Waked.

His wife carried out his request, and with her two children left
the country: from Rashayya to Beirut, and from there onboard a
steamship to Canada.

103

A year after the family arrived, a third son was born and they called
him Saleem (safe) in auspicious recognition of their safe arrival and
the reunion of the family. Saleem, later known among friends as
Sam, was Mu'een's father. He grew up in Canada, completing his
secondary education. His father then made Saleem go to work and
he opened a grocery store for him where he spent much of his time.
Later Saleem was attracted to the real estate business. He threw himself into this wholeheartedly and was very successful.

The business was carried on by his four children who inherited
his honesty, fear of God and obedience to the law. The Waked Real
Estate Company became the most important real estate company
on the Island and opened branches in a couple other cities. His son
Ted (Tawfeeq) moved to Halifax where he managed a branch; Chuck
(Shakeeb) took a branch of the company to Montreal; Elizabeth separated herself from the family business by marriage; and Mu'een remained his father's right-hand man.

When his father entered the municipal elections and won a
councilor's seat, Mu'een was his greatest help. His success marked
a changing point in the relations between immigrants and the people
of this country, for the occasion drew attention to the good position
the immigrants had reached through hard work, effort, honesty and
integrity.

Immigrants on the Island began to date events by Councilor
Saleem's period, classifying themselves as before, during or after
the Councilor's term of office.

The Councilor had been invited to lunch with the two guests from the homeland, and his son had almost forgotten the appointment.

104

"In a few minutes, Mu'een will be back with his father," Lamya said as she brought her mother a drink. She then prepared her father's favorite: "lion's milk" or *arak*. She started to get drinks for her husband and his father, but when Mu'een returned, he took over, leaving Lamya to get the lunch ready

"Lunch is served," she finally announced. "Uncle, Mother, Father: please honor our table."

The dinner table was laden with food. Uncle Saleem seemed quite pleased to be here and asked questions nonstop. How were the general conditions of the homeland? What had happened to Rashayya? Had the war of the south reached it? Rashayya's name had kept cropping up in the newscasts.

Radwan told him that the Rashayya of the news was Rashayya al-Fukhar.

"What difference does it make, Abu Nabeel," Saleem said, "whether they are bombing Rashayya al-Fukhar or Rashayyaa-Wadi, Jurat Al-Sindyan, Beirut or Sidon? The arrow is one and the same. Our hearts jump into our mouths at every newscast. I've not let a single occasion pass without sending protest letters or corrections. They even pronounce the names wrong. They make mistakes when naming locations and the different factions involved. In the latest newscast I heard, they said that foreigners were being evacuated. This means that the situation in Lebanon is extremely dangerous. And then there are endless rumors."

Radwan listened to the venerable man. He appreciated his interest in the affairs of the homeland, in spite of the fact that he was born here, in Canada, and had seen Lebanon only once. He had visited the village in search of a bride and had returned with Summary. Summary had died three years earlier and had left him an old man suffering from heart trouble. However, he remained alert and strong-willed, and capably managed the affairs of the Lebanese immigrants who swore by his name and sang his praises.

Radwan already knew all that from the homeland. For news traveled, both the good and the bad, in letters and with those returning to visit. And he had repeatedly expressed pride that his daughter Lamya had become an in law of this distinguished family.

Now he was facing Saleem for the first time, listening to him talk in a simple, humble and good-hearted tone. He spoke with an enthusiasm which could not have been good for his sick heart, though he stopped to take a deep breath at the end of every sentence.

When Radwan heard the Councilor speak of rumors, he became curious.

"What rumors, Uncle Saleem? Tell us."

"They throw different news at us every day," he responded. "Lebanon will become a battlefield. There is an international conspiracy whose dimensions nobody knows. They've chosen Lebanon as its theater. But Canada, as far as I know, is not party to this conspiracy because our Prime Minister is an intelligent man. He insists that this country should not succumb to America's pressure, whenever possible. We also heard, Abu Nabeel, that the government of Canada might open the doors to Lebanese immigration. Some people are even saying that Canada is preparing special areas for these immigrants to live. But I think this is only a rumor and I don't believe it. Opening Canada to immigration is reasonable. It is done for humanitarian reasons, and because there are a lot of Lebanese immigrants in Canada, the government might be doing this to please them. Everyone who has a sister, brother, father, mother or wife in Lebanon will not abandon them and leave them exposed to danger."

Radwan listened, and he listened well. He had drunk his first glass of arak and poured a second without eating a mouthful of food. His eyes were fixed on the lips of the Councilor so that he would not miss a single word of prophecy.

The Councilor knew what was happening in Canada more than most people, because of his connections with political circles and because he read the newspapers. He also knew what was happening in Lebanon, because of his emotional ties to the homeland. Radwan felt that he was ignorant of what had been happening around him, what was being done to his country, to his land. It was true that the rounds of fighting had begun before he left. But he did not believe, along with many other citizens, that these "rounds" could turn into a devastating, crushing war that would cause the population — in particular the young ones — to flee.

105

He began to feel guilty about his own lack of knowledge.

Why, man, why are you trying to avoid the facts? You saw them before you left, at the airport, at the airline office — long lines of young men forced to flee, to escape. You also saw them standing at the road blocks, with weapons in their hands and fire in their eyes. What did these young men intend to do? Throw a party? Wake up, man. You were — and still are — asleep. Wake up !

Lamya's voice startled him. "Why aren't you eating, Father? I cooked the fish just for you."

He smiled at her. He tried to drive away the clouds that fogged his eyes and his heart, and to speak clearly so that his words would not show the confusion inside him.

"I'm eating. But you know, I always like to nurse my drink. You've forgotten your father's habits, sweet one."

Lamya had not forgotten. She gave him a small bit to eat, which he took, thanking her. The change that had come over his face and to his eyes did not escape her. She knew what he was thinking, and she also knew the surprise which she and her brothers and sister had prepared for their father. But they would keep it a secret until the right time came.

106

Supper at Nabeel's house was an occasion for which the entire family gathered, along with friends.

Nabeel had a special ritual to his invitations: he would first decide that supper was to be at his house, then he would inform his wife, Salma. She would prepare the food together with all the women who would later be present. Nabeel would invite his guests by telephone, one by one. "Supper is at our house tonight. Please do come!"

In the evening he would leave his store early, come home and change his clothes. He would go into the kitchen alone to prepare the raw kibbi, the taratur, the tabbouli and other dishes he was so good at. Rich with spices and herbs, the original flavors were preserved — the kibbi made in the stone mortar at Jurat Al-Sindyan, the tabbouli salad prepared in the Hasbani restaurants. In addition to these dishes, he would serve a plate of fried fresh-water fish which he had caught himself with his favorite fishing rod, whenever the weather permitted. Only cold weather that drove the fish to deeper water deprived him of his favorite hobby.

Shihadeh al-Asmar was among the invited guests. He could not take his eyes off the fish and kept asking, "Where and when did you catch such fish?" and "How dare you go fishing without telling me?" and "Is this our agreement, my friend?"

Nabeel let him ask all the questions he wanted. He took pleasure in goading him into making further comments. Such dialogues ended, on most occasions, with Shihadeh's silence or his disgruntled exit.

The guests knew Shihadeh's soft spot, for he could not bear being left behind on a fishing trip. The subject had become one for jokes and teasing.

Shihadeh suffered a lot this particular evening, because Nabeel had obviously not asked him to go along. To make things worse, Nabeel had invited Shihadeh to taste the fruits of his exclusion.

107

Nabeel did not purposely avoid Shihadeh. It was only that his time did not allow him to plan ahead for his fishing trips. He would be at his store when the desire for fishing suddenly hit like an inspiration. He would leave work, hurry home, put on his fishing clothes and rubber waders. He would hook up his boat to the car, take his fishing rod and go.

Where?

To rivers which ran so slowly that an outsider would think they were only streams or frozen swamps, in which all kinds of shrubs and thorny bushes intertwined. He would pull his boat into the water. Usually, one of his brothers or his eldest son, Rudy, would accompany him. Nabeel had taught Rudy to fish when he was only six.

He would cast his line and forget about time and all the pressures of work. He would focus on the point where his line disappeared into the water. His only concern was whether a fish bit, whether one ate the bait and got caught, or somehow escaped the hook and swam to deeper water to rub its damaged mouth on the weeds.

The hours fishing passed quickly. The sun would set, darkness would fall. But the fish did not sleep and the passion for fishing did not subside. Hunger and sleepiness were held at bay, and the fisherman would remember not to catch more than the number permitted by law. Every fisherman could only catch twenty. And woe to him who broke the law! His license would be taken away and he would have to pay a heavy fine.

A man of Lebanese origin, coming from the villages of the north or south, would be alone in those vast open spaces. There would be no one to watch or count. There would be nobody calling to him save the birds, secure in their nests deep in the heart of the dark forest. The Lebanese man would be alone, yet he would feel the law had arms that could reach him wherever he went, secret eyes that observed him from inside like the Creator's. His conscience would tremble and the Lebanese man would abandon his natural disposition to nonchalance. He would not dream about disobeying the law and would be satisfied with twenty little fish, or even less if the fish were not biting.

This was what Nabeel, his brothers and his friends would do. Even Shihadeh, known for his insatiable greed, would leave the river after catching the legal limit.

108

This evening, Shihadeh was a guest invited in honor of an old friend, Radwan Abu Yusef. He took advantage of the occasion.

"Nabeel," he said, "your father and I have agreed to go fishing together."

He pronounced his words clearly and smiled slyly. He felt he was in charge.

Nabeel saw through his ruse and immediately welcomed the suggestion. "You're welcome, on condition you get up early."

"What?" Shihadeh exclaimed in surprise. He did not believe that Nabeel had so quickly accepted his suggestion. "Are we going tomorrow?"

"Yes," Nabeel answered. "If the weather is suitable, we'll take Abu Nabeel on a fishing trip before the ice arrives."

Radwan's joy and excitement were no less than Shihadeh's. He leapt from his chair.

"I must get ready! I've not brought my fishing clothes with me!"

Nabeel tried to calm him. "Everything is ready, Father — the clothes and the rubber waders. We'll go in the morning after we get a good night's sleep."

109

Sleep?

Since when could Radwan sleep on a night of such a great invitation? Furthermore, fishing was going to be in unknown territory. He was eager, especially since he had not fished in a long time. Fishing and hunting had become mere memories.

For many years now he had not used a fishing rod, a net or a gun. He had been content with staying inside or with sitting on the porch outside.

Before the war in South Lebanon, he used to carry his double-barreled shotgun and go to the hills of al-'Urqoob and to the vineyards and olive groves. In recent years he did not dare carry even a stick to lean on when he was tired. He was afraid they might mistake it for a gun and chase him from the air or from the observation points surrounding Jurat Al-Sindyan.

The unexpected invitation filled him with anticipation.

110

Radwan did not hear the rest of Nabeel's words. He got up. "We'll rest a little until dawn. Have a good night, everyone," he said.

Shihadeh got up and prepared to leave. That was a sign for everyone to disperse, each to his own home, in order to have a little sleep and rest before the new work day began.

111

"I can't get over the fact that you're here, Abu Nabeel! I can hardly believe it!"

Shihadeh had even forgotten to say good morning. He bobbed with excitement. "Who would ever believe, my dear brother, Radwan, that we'd be together on this Island on a fishing trip, just like in the old days? God bless the good old days!"

His head looked like a cabbage. Nothing but two holes were showing — his vigilant eyes. He turned to Nabeel.

"Those were the days, Nabeel. Those were the days of our youth, before you and your generation."

Nabeel did not answer. His mind was preoccupied as it leapt ahead of the car, trying to plan the trip and determine which streams would make for better fishing at this time of year.

Radwan sat silently next to Nabeel, his eyes on the road, their red color betraying the fact that he had not slept.

Nabeel noticed his eyes as he gave him a cup of coffee from the thermos.

"Didn't you sleep, Father?"

"We slept a little," Radwan muttered.

"It doesn't show in your eyes! Next time I won't tell you when we're going!"

"The truth, Nabeel, is that I could not sleep," Radwan admitted to his son. "What happened to me, I don't know. I only know that I haven't been so sleepless for a long time. I can't say this hasn't happened since my childhood, because my childhood days did not know any happy surprises. You may say, Son, that I was sleepless last night because of extreme joy and excitement."

Shihadeh interrupted. "That is what happened to me too, Abu Nabeel. Is it possible that men our age lie awake at night like a child thinking of the birthday gift they would receive in the morning?"

112

This gift was different, though: it was cunning, it hid behind rocks, in the depths of the streams, in the thick shrubs, in the roots of the willows...

"Here, Father. This is your fishing rod, and here is the bag of bait."

"What shall I do?"

"Stay in the boat and cast your line from it."

"As for me," Shihadeh said, "I'll be a little ways away."

Nabeel teased, "Of course you won't be right here. The fish are waiting for you at the Shihadeh Stream."

Radwan laughed at the joke. "Good for you, Brother Shihadeh! Already there's a stream named after you!"

Shihadeh did not answer. He had moved away and began wading into the water, crossing it as if he were an aquatic creature who spent all his life in rivers and streams. He soon disappeared as Nabeel's voice followed him.

"Don't go very far, Uncle Shihadeh, in case we lose you. Don't make us worry about you!"

Shihadeh did not hear. He continued wading. Perhaps he was dreaming that he was wading in a river which had embraced him in his boyhood, known his childish acts, and accompanied him as a sincere friend during his youth and early manhood.

That river was far away now.

It was too far even for dreams.

113

Dawn was breaking. The day was spreading slowly, flowing from a silver-grey sky. It brought with it an icy dampness, the breath of the North Pole.

Radwan was ready for all possibilities. He sat in the boat holding his fishing rod and waited, a serious look on his face.

Nabeel went to a stream a short distance from the boat after he weighed anchor and tied the boat firmly to a strong tree trunk, assured that his father was comfortable and relaxed.

Relaxed?

Radwan had not relaxed since the previous evening. The mere promise of the fishing trip had kept him in suspense and stolen away his sleep. How much more would the trip itself do?

He now waited for the fish to bite. He remembered past fishing trips and indulged himself in the warmth of memories, forgetting the cold surrounding him. Suddenly, his line shook, and he jerked it and reeled it in quickly. His heart rejoiced like a child's when he saw a fish struggling on the line. He took it off the hook, and put it in the knapsack. That was the first blessing.

One after another, the fish bit and the joy went to his head, intoxicating him and making him forget his two companions. He heard the fish still struggling inside the knapsack.

His heart was full as his lips repeated, "Praise be to Him who made it not a sin to kill you!"

He apologized to the fish. "Please forgive us. It's only a short trip we're on. We'll not be here every day."

He suddenly remembered what Nabeel had said. "Don't catch more than ten fish."

When he had asked why only ten, when the number permitted by law was twenty, Nabeel answered, "True, the number is twenty. But the law doesn't permit fishing without a license. So if you stop at ten, I'll be able to catch ten fish myself. You'll have fished on my license."

Radwan shook his head with disapproval.

"I really don't understand these complications, Son. The river is full of fish and they bite with greed, and yet we are expected to sit with folded arms, just watching? I don't think this is right!"

"Perhaps it is not right, Father. But this is the law of the land. Next time I'll get you a license and you can fish as you like."

114

He raised his knapsack to look inside. He counted. The number exceeded ten. He had disobeyed his son's instructions by two fish. He felt he had committed an offense for which he should be punished. The matter was no longer related to fish and fishing, but to his son Nabeel's approval and compliance with the law.

He sat up to look at his surroundings, and his eyes moved toward the trees behind which Shihadeh had disappeared. He listened but did not hear a sound. Not a branch moved. Shihadeh must be deeply involved in fishing. This must be what tied his friend so strongly to this land. If it were not for these streams and rivers, the man would not have been able to live in a society totally unrelated to him in any way. The stream returned him to his youth, to the Hasbani River.

The young men who teased Shihadeh the night before had not realized his strong need for this.

He decided to tell his son. "Son, you've all kinds of ties that connect you with this country. You speak the language, you're successful in your work, you're married and have children — may God protect them from evil eyes. But Shihadeh's case is very difficult. You should make life easy for him as long as he is unable to return to Dair Mimas."

He decided he would say all this to Nabeel and other things too. Suddenly, he saw the reeds and the willow branches opposite him moving. He did not see any contours of a human being, so he thought it might be an animal hiding in the bushes. He wondered what kind of animal it could be, which plunged deep into the water and shook the trees from their roots.

Then he saw the cabbage head floating on the surface of the water. Radwan recognized his friend Shihadeh who was wading amid the reeds and bushes. The water went up almost to his neck.

"Shihadeh, take care lest you drown!" he shouted.

Shihadeh waved his hand. "Don't be afraid, Abu Nabeel. Your face brings good luck!"

"How many fish have you caught?" Radwan yelled.

"God's bounty is abundant...."

<h2 style="text-align:center">115</h2>

He did not tell him how many. Nabeel heard the dialogue from where he was standing. He hurried to the boat carrying the fish he caught. His face was beaming.

"Have you been successful?" was the first question he asked his father.

"Yes, thank God," Radwan said softly.

"I mean, how many fish?" he insisted.

His father looked like a child who had been caught red-handed. "As many as you said—plus two."

Nabeel did not seem annoyed, so Radwan went on. "Fishing is tempting, Son. I thought I had caught only five or six. But when I looked into the knapsack, I was surprised—I started counting. After I counted ten, there were two more at the bottom of the knapsack!"

Nabeel laughed merrily. "I thought this might happen. So I only caught seven. You can still catch one more."

"Let's have less rather than more, Son. Greed is bad. The important thing now is to know how many fish Shihadeh has caught."

"Shihadeh! You're looking for the impossible, Abu Nabeel! Shihadeh hides the fish in his trousers so that we won't know the real number!"

Radwan laughed and the echo of his laughter reached Shihadeh's ears.

"Brother Radwan," he shouted, "you're laughing at me, aren't you?"

"Not at all," retorted Radwan. "I'm laughing at Nabeel's joke."

"Nabeel? Do you think he has nothing better to do than joke about Shihadeh?"

Radwan tried to defend his son. "We were only wondering how many fish you'd caught. In fact, Nabeel convinced me not to ask you such a question."

Shihadeh was encouraged. "I hide no secrets from you, Abu Nabeel. I caught a dozen, plus this string." He held up the evidence.

"You can't deceive us, Shihadeh," Nabeel teased. "What about your pockets? Why do you think they're bulging?"

Shihadeh's hand moved automatically to his pockets as he muttered, "It's only water. I swear by this very blessing, it's only water."

Nabeel ended the dialogue. "God bless your catch. It's yours to keep. We were only teasing you, Uncle Shihadeh. Come on, let's go."

The three men went into the water, raised the boat and carried it to the main road. Nabeel hooked it to his car and they returned to the city, oblivious to the surprise that awaited them.

116

This was Canada.

Foggy air, endless green and yellow plains and gigantic forests.

The trees rose to the sky, to their Creator. They intertwined, shoulder to shoulder, so that the sun's rays could not filter through. The trees lived in darkness and desolation for many months.

The eye then leapt to rivers and lakes and quiet marshes.

This was nature in all its might and power.

But where was man?

Who planted the plains? Who guarded the forests? Who dared disturb the quiet, penetrate the darkness, and enter into its heart to explore its mysteries and decipher its symbols?

Radwan wondered at all this, looking around in amazement like a child going for his first walk in the wilderness.

He was no stranger to this life.

He had grown up in it. He was indeed a child of the wilderness.

But nature here was not like the one he knew, where the olive trees comforted him, the vines stretched out their arms to welcome him, and the willows bent down until their tops caressed the surface of the earth.

There, in his warm little village, he felt he could stretch out his hand and hold the vineyard, the garden and the wheat fields in his palm. He could grasp the vast distances between one footstep and the next.

Here...who knew where these plains stretched? Who took care of them? Who planted and harvested them?

117

The earth could not bear to be neglected. It could not be left to waste, left for thorns to overrun it. The earth was precious in his homeland, very precious. A man would die for a square foot of it.

Ever since Radwan had first opened his eyes, he had witnessed how people clung to their land, to every grain of soil, to every little orchard and hillside terrace.

They put landmarks on the boundaries like guards, and woe to the one who strayed one step inside his neighbor's territory.

The land was transferred from generation to generation, sons inheriting it from their fathers as they had from their fathers before them. The caravan of time marched on in a continuous line, uninterrupted by any obstacle, unstopped by any wall.

Yet here, the land was endless...like the grey sky that hung over it.

He turned to his son and asked, "Who owns this land, Nabeel?"

"It used to belong to the government, Father. But now most of the land is private property. When someone came forward and offered to cultivate a piece of forest, he was encouraged to do so, sometimes with the help of grants and loans."

The idea that the state encouraged development appealed to Radwan.

"God bless this country!" Radwan said, as though he wanted Canada to hear out loud his opinion of the country. "This type of encouragement builds a real civilization. God bless it!"

"But what happens, Father," Nabeel continued, "is that some people take advantage of it—"

"I don't blame them," Shihadeh interrupted. "So long as the government takes care of everything, why should they have to work? And you mustn't forget the weather. The weather here is horrible, Abu Nabeel."

Nabeel went on. "Every day, the government attempts to overcome the difficulties of nature. Take travel, for example. The Island used to be almost cut off from the world in the wintertime. Today, there are ships that break the ice and move between the Island and the mainland. Airplanes don't stop flying, no matter how severe the weather might be. Even the ocean — which used to frighten people when it froze — has been turned into a place for dancing and horse racing."

"What are you saying, Nabeel?" the question leapt to Radwan's lips. "You're right to be surprised," he answered. "I'm not joking, Father. In two months we'll take you to see skating and horse racing on the surface of the sea."

"This is a miracle! Dancing on the sea? Horse racing on the ice? This is truly a land of wonders!"

"It is, indeed," Nabeel said. "And every day, the wonders increase in the hands of people who are always ready to face difficulties and challenges. Canada's weather has been the greatest challenge to man as he continues expanding towards the north."

But this expansion has been so slow," Shihadeh objected. "For a hundred years now, the population on this Island has hardly increased at all."

"Does this mean people aren't interested in the Island, Shihadeh?" Radwan wanted to know.

"Brother Abu Nabeel, people are like sunflowers: wherever the sun turns, they follow it. The population here is 130,000 at the most. That means their number is equal to that of only one of Beirut's neighborhoods, although its area is almost the same as that of Mount Lebanon."

Nabeel added, "For this reason, the government encourages people to spread out into the empty areas. At any rate, we are a thousand times better off on this Island than people further north."

Shihadeh nodded his head mockingly. "Lucky us! People further north. Does this mean we are in the south?"

118

Radwan listened. He was trying to understand and to learn everything about the life his children led in this strange country. He wanted to reassure himself and carry back to Lebanon something to sustain him in the long winter nights ahead.

From this short dialogue he could better understand what the Councilor had said about the Canadian government's facilities for Lebanese immigrants, who, because of the recent circumstances in the homeland, were made homeless or killed, and suffered the tragedy of war.

As a consequence, he came upon a problem for which he could not find a solution. Which was better: remain in one's homeland and be subjected to all kinds of humiliation and torture, even death, or emigrate to another country where one suffers from the cold and the constant yearning for one's homeland?

He remembered that that had been the situation of his compatriots for a long time. He remembered his brothers and sister who had chosen to emigrate. He thought of his own children who had followed the same path several decades later. Thinking of this subject increased his anxiety. It almost made him forget that he was returning from a successful fishing trip carrying a knapsack full of fish, and that Um Nabeel would be waiting for him, as she had always done. He turned to his left and looked at the face of Nabeel, the most beloved of his children. This man was Radwan's main support now, the source of his future security.

He heard Shihadeh mutter, "We're there. Thank you, my dear Nabeel. I wish you the best on every fishing trip in the future, Brother Radwan."

Radwan was back in the city. Within a few minutes he got out of the car carrying his knapsack, proof of his successful trip.

As he had guessed, Um Nabeel was at the door, welcoming him home, her face overflowing with joy. "Hurry, Abu Nabeel. Raji has just arrived from N'York."

119

Raji was her brother.

When Raji left the homeland, his sister Raya was just a baby. They had not seen each other since the day he closed the door behind him, never looking back.

He emigrated, like her sister Almas had done, and did not think of returning all these years. But as soon as he heard that Um Nabeel was in Canada, he hurried to see her. Um Nabeel could hardly contain herself. She took her husband by the hand and led him to the bathroom.

"Wash yourself, husband, and change your clothes. Raji is in the sitting room."

Nabeel could hardly believe his ears. "Uncle Raji is here? A thousand times welcome!"

He rushed to embrace him. The uncle wept and his warm tears flowed down his cheeks. They were tears of joy at the reunion and tears of regret at the years of separation.

What had Raji been waiting for?

He himself did not know. Days had passed: difficult overwhelming days which had cast him into a whirlpool of work. The wheel turned: he was caught and was spinning round and round. He could not get out, and the wheel did not stop, until Nabeel called him on the telephone.

"Uncle, I have good news for you. My parents have arrived from the homeland. We hope you'll honor us with your presence."

Raji wanted desperately to hear his sister's voice, but his words faltered. What would he tell her? What would he say after a separation of six decades?

When he left Jurat Al-Sindyan, Raya was a child with fair hair, rosy cheeks and honey-colored eyes. She was an intelligent and cheerful little girl.

What would he say on embracing a seventy-year-old woman when he himself was pushing eighty?

Could he believe she was his sister and he was her brother? What had they known of fraternal love apart from the letters exchanged across the seas—the letters that conveyed feelings of yearning and longing, and complaints about the anguish of separation?

120

"My dear sister Raya, stay near me, dear one. Sit down, don't tire yourself, don't keep moving. I've missed you, I've missed you so much."

He enfolded her in his arms as though, in this one person, he was holding his mother, his land and his country.

Radwan entered while they were holding each other and was embarrassed. This was the first time he had seen Um Nabeel in anyone else's arms but his.

He knew the man was her brother. But in spite of himself, he felt the sharp bite of jealousy gnawing at his heart.

Where did her brother come from?

From years of separation!

He used to be a picture on the wall, words in letters, a name in memories. Now he was present, in body, before his eyes. He was a handsome man in spite of his eighty years. He had a strong build and a beaming and lively face that had the same features as hers.

This stranger was her brother!

He came forward, shook hands and embraced him. He noticed Raji's questioning eyes and searching looks. He felt that the brother had come now, after half a century, in order to approve or disapprove of their marriage.

He sat opposite this man, trying to hide his discomfort. He did not know how to talk to him. So he lit up a cigarette and listened. Um Nabeel seemed far away from him.

All of a sudden, she became Raya, daughter of Tawfeeq Abu Nijim who lived in Jurat Al-Sindyan, and he was Radwan Abu Yusef, the miller who fell in love with her at first sight and spent long sleepless nights dreaming of her beautiful eyes.

Here was her brother now, coming to approve or object half a century after the fact, after the children had grown into married adults, after he had become a grandfather and she a grandmother sixteen times over. Now the grey hair crowned her head and the wrinkles invaded her rosy face and surrounded her honey-colored eyes.

Here was her brother, after sixty years of absence. "Welcome to you, my brother-in-law! I was very eager to get acquainted with you, Abu Nabeel. I've heard good things about you but circumstances have prevented us from meeting before now."

Radwan collected his courage. "This is the happiest moment of my life, my dear Abu Raymond. We've lived many years thinking of you and speaking about you. We often dreamed we'd meet you one day. Thank God, the dream has finally come true."

"It will be even better when you both come to New York and get to know my family. My sister Almas is also waiting for you. It is too difficult for Almas to travel."

121

Radwan had siblings in New York. Their names he knew by heart: Yusef, Saad and Adla. What if one of them were to appear now and embrace him — get to know him after this long life of separation and dreams? But where were the siblings? Were they dead or alive?

Since the war in 1914, he had heard nothing about them. They were lost in a city called New York. The giant city had swallowed them. Since he had first become aware of life around him, he had heard that they had gone to New York and never returned.

The subject was not forgotten. As soon as he set foot in Canada, he had asked about them. First he asked Nabeel.

"Have you tried, my son, to find out about your Uncle Saad, your Uncle Yusef and your Aunt Adla?"

Nabeel had asked often, and his inquiries reached his Uncle Raji and his Aunt Almas.

"No one has heard anything about them, Father. Most probably they changed their names or they moved. They went to New York before the First World War, but who can confirm that they stayed there?"

Nabeel heard other words repeated in his consciousness.

"N'York? They all used to travel to N'York. The city came to mean all places of emigration. N'York to the people who live in it is just a city. But in the eyes that waited and the hearts that trembled in the villages of the homeland, N'York meant eternal alienation, estrangement, loss...."

His father carried his old faith and the permanent question. He posed it to Raji.

"My dear Abu Raymond, have you ever heard anything about my brothers Saad and Yusef, and my sister Adla? They emigrated to N'York a long time ago, before the 1914 war. They left and never wrote."

"Nabeel spoke to me about this some time ago, and I looked for them. I asked other immigrants, I searched the telephone directory, I inquired at club meetings. Unfortunately, I did not have any luck."

"Does this mean we should consider them lost?" Radwan asked in despair.

"There are many like them, Abu Nabeel. Who knows? Perhaps we'll hear good news about them when you visit us."

Radwan said resignedly, "May God listen to you...and protect your children."

Raji's words brought back Radwan's confidence and revived his hopes. Who knows? A miracle may happen and he may find them, exactly as a miracle had happened in Raji's life.

122

Memory travels across time like mythical birds.

It takes flight from reality, flaps its wings, and soars faraway, crossing the gates of years, penetrating the folds of darkness to dig into the past....

123

Raji came in from the past. Until now he had been a mere picture on a wall, words in a letter. His was an old story that climbed up Radwan's life as the bramble would climb up the trunk of a poplar tree, wrapping and clothing it so that nothing but the rustle of leaves would remain.

Radwan had set off on this flight against his time and his days, even against the direction of his memory. He had not prepared himself for surprises. Yet, whenever he stretched out his hand to open a door, a new world opened up before his eyes, arousing in him the wonder of a child. Whenever a new face showed up, the streams of the past and the flow of time rushed through his veins.

Time was not content with the wrinkles and folds it drew upon his forehead, in his sinking cheeks and around his eyes. It was now taking him to a new tunnel and placing him face to face with this myth emerging from the mirage of days. He stood still and remembered. He imprinted the scene in his memory as proof that he had truly witnessed what he was seeing and hearing, so that if he should one day sit on his porch with his friends, he would have no doubts that it had really happened. He would persuade his listeners: "I'm telling you, friends, God has so graciously extended my life that I was able to travel to N'York and see Raji, my brother-in-law and Um Nabeel's brother. Praise be to the Creator who provides, for He has indeed provided for Raji!"

124

Raji had left his mark before he emigrated from Jurat Al-Sindyan. But that was a long time ago. Days passed and fell one after another like autumn leaves that were then covered by the soil under the trees of the village. But they infiltrated the sap of the trees and appeared as shining fruits hanging from the branches.

In those days the young men of Jurat Al-Sindyan experienced *safarbarlek*, a type of military conscription during the Ottoman rule, when despotism was at its peak. Young men were ripped away from their fathers and mothers, from the earth that embraced them and nourished them, and were cast into the unknown.

From Jurat Al-Sindyan, a flock of nestlings was swept up and Raji was one of them.

What did they do to him?

What happened in that dark period of time?

Nobody remembered. Nobody wanted to remember.

Radwan learned the story after Raji returned from that trip.

He had returned as a deserter fleeing hunger and misery, though he could not flee sickness. One dark night he knocked at his parents' door. His mother did not recognize him and his father stood there tongue-tied. When they recovered from their shock at his ravaged appearance, they hid him in a hut on the outskirts of the village.

125

Raji lay unconscious in the hut for two weeks. His mother never left his side, kneeling at his feet, patiently dripping water between his parched lips and trying to cure his sickness with compresses of vinegar and alcohol. And she prayed.

Like Raji, she was unconscious in her trance of fervent prayers. She was in that distant world of dreams when a stranger came to her. His appearance was awesome: his hair and beard were grey, he walked barefoot and wore a white cloak.

"Who are you, sir?" she asked in amazement.

"I am the doctor," he answered. "Give your son this water to drink." He pointed to a brass bowl which she usually used for drinking.

As her eyes sought the brass bowl, the stranger disappeared and she awakened from her trance.

Without wasting another moment, she hurried to the bowl and found that it had some water in it. She took it and began dripping it into her son's mouth. As she gave him the last drop, Raji opened his eyes.

"Mother, where am I?"

She embraced him in disbelief. "You're in your mother's heart, my love."

"Please give me something to drink, Mother."

She gave him water, rubbed away the sweat trickling down his forehead and wiped his eyes with the edge of a soft white cloth.

"I am healed, Mother."

"I know that, Son. The doctor has just visited us and healed you."

The sick man opened his eyes in fear. "The doctor? Where is the doctor? Did the soldiers come in?"

"No, no. Don't be afraid, my dear one. The doctor is not the soldiers. He was sent to us by Divine Power."

Raji's mother was sure it was her faith that called on the doctor in a dream. And a miracle had happened, a miracle of faith and motherly sacrifice. She did not speak with Raji about this matter until several days after he was fully healed. She waited until he recovered his strength, was able to walk around the room and eat his meals by himself. Then she told him about the stranger's visit, which she described in great detail.

"Mother," he said, "your faith has healed me. I'll remain a man of faith all my life."

The young man was sure that a miracle had happened and brought him back from the grave. Fever was cutting down young men: he had seen them before he escaped from the army. They died on the roadside, and were left in the open for wild beasts and birds of prey.

He had been dying and yet he lived. But he knew he could not stay in his country, and his father knew that too.

After he regained his health, the father gave him some money and smuggled him out with a group of young men who were emigrating. The young men were headed for Sidon. The trip took them three days—they walked at night and hid during the day. When they arrived, Raji was barefoot and his clothes were in tatters. He looked no different than most travelers of the day.

He bought a ticket and was loaded on board a cargo ship going to Marseilles, which was the port where all emigrants had to stop. Travelers met there before their paths separated. Each one of them was heading for an unknown destination. Their only concern was to get out of the country and escape the tyranny of the rulers.

Raji knew where he was going: to New York where his uncles and others from his village lived. In his hand he carried a paper with several names and addresses. In his heart he carried the treasured faith of his mother.

"Son," she had said as he was leaving, "God wanted you to live when He saved you from the safarbarlek, and when He delivered you from fever and the spies lying in wait all around us. Go, my son, and let contentment and faith be the companions of your path in life."

126

And so Raji found himself on board a steamship, among a herd of humans being driven away by the storms of injustice which had carried away his uncles before him. He was continuing their journey, following their footsteps as the September birds followed their line of migration, year after year, season after season.

He did not count the days of his journey, nor did he record it in his memory. In fact, he pulled out those days and cast them into the sea as soon as the ship dropped anchor in the New York harbor.

He arrived into a world submerged in fog and desolation.

He carried his bundle of belongings and went to search for his uncles' home.

127

Sixty years had passed since Raji arrived in New York.

Six decades...a lifetime!

Oh, how fast life passed!

He was now over eighty! But light still shone in his face and tenderness radiated from his eyes. It was that kind of warmth which instantly lifted you from the land of cold and carried you to the village of olives, grapes and figs in the south of Lebanon.

Sixty long, heavy and uncharted years had not been able to erase those wonderful features, which the young man carried from his small village to one of the biggest cities in the world, New York.

It was from New York that he had come to see his sister and meet his brother-in-law, and to invite them both to visit.

128

Radwan was elated at the invitation.

New York to him had been a myth, a mere summer night's dream. It was a name that grew larger and larger on his lips, until his imagination could no longer contain it. The name came closer to him, calmly and tenderly. It approached Radwan's hearing, then his entire being, and it enveloped him.

Radwan was going to New York!

He was going to travel, to penetrate the impossible, to perform the miracle. He would touch it with his own hands, with his cracked palms...touch it with a heart full of love for life and wonder at all existence, with a heart that carried to this strange world all the dreams and hopes of the past.

129

Radwan had become used to air travel. His first flight had made him an experienced passenger. Now here he was, walking with bold, sure steps, followed by his life's companion, Um Nabeel, who was leaning on Lamya's arm.

It had fallen upon Lamya to accompany her parents to New York. The young men had their businesses to run, Nawal was tied up with teaching at the university, and Mu'een volunteered to take his wife's place at home, doing the housework and taking care of the children.

Radwan landed in New York. His trip to the New World would not be complete until he visited the city which to him was the symbol of all emigration.

The airport was nothing out of the ordinary, like all the airports that had received him. The employees were similar, the strange faces were strange, even the beautiful hostesses did not arouse his interest. He had become accustomed to seeing blonde hair, white faces and graceful bodies. Seeing one of those young women made him feel like he had seen them all.

Besides, there was a more important thing than these appearances. Side paths were not going to distract him from the main road leading to the magical city.

As a child's imagination would emerge from the depths of legendary stories, forgetting everything else, so began Radwan's discovery of the city.

130

"It's New York, Father...."

Lamya was trying to explain. He would listen to her for a few moments, then the ever-changing scene would steal away his attention and increase his wonder and amazement.

This was New York.

He was looking at it from this wide avenue, from a car window which limited his vision and did not allow his imagination to fly.

"May God's name be praised! Lamya, what a world!"

He then turned to Um Nabeel as though he had just realized that she was still by his side.

"Look, look, wife! It's N'York! Who would ever have believed it? We're in the heart of N'York!"

A wide smile spread over his face, radiating from his eyes. Its brilliance was reflected on all that surrounded him.

His eyes jumped eagerly, surveying the shop windows, the human beings crawling on the sidewalks, those entering and leaving everywhere.

His ears absorbed the hum of the city where the sound of the machine was louder than that of man. The machine rose like a giant. Next to it man appeared like a creeping insect. Yet it was from the brains of this insect that buildings, skyscrapers, suspension bridges and all the wonders of architecture emerged.

The luxurious American car wound its way along the paved roads, well-acquainted with the ins and outs of the city. The car knew its way, yet if Radwan were to spend a couple of lifetimes here, he could never learn how to move around.

131

He withdrew into his inner world.

How are you going to know, man? How are you going to find your way in these labyrinths, in this wide world where buildings embrace one another like trees in a forest, where streets interconnect and never separate, and can carry you to the unknown?

Aren't you afraid of being lost, man?

It's here that three of your own flesh and blood have been lost: Saad, Yusef and Adla. They entered the city several decades before you. They were full of eagerness and questions and hopes for the future — and the city swallowed them.

Which streets took them?

Where do they live?

How are you to know? These roads intertwine, separate, wind and turn around the trunks of the buildings, leaving no space for the imagination to rest or any oasis where the emotions can have a siesta when the sun is at its peak.

132

Radwan wiped away tears that, in spite of himself, had rolled down his cheeks.

"Looking makes me tired," he muttered. "How can one ever cope with seeing all of this world?"

His eyes grew lively again and resumed their eager search into this amazing scene. They tried to open a small window so he could have a dialogue with this city...just an opening the size of one's palm, like the one through which the employee at the Canadian Consulate in Beirut had spoken to him and through which had sprung his first trip into this world of wonder and amazement.

After he had stood there in that long line waiting patiently and silently before the Consulate employee, Radwan could no longer find himself. Like a butterfly that leaves the solitude of its cocoon, his old self left him and fluttered about, sometimes madly and sometimes calmly, sometimes in complete surrender.

There was no time now for surrender!

As the car entered the gate to the garden, he said quietly to himself, you have no time to meditate, man. You have no time to dream. You're living the most exciting moments of our life. Look and store up images to show them later on, when you return to Jurat Al-Sindyan. When everybody comes to welcome you back, from the lower quarter, the eastern quarter, the upper quarter, and from the neighboring houses. They will come to see you in groups — men, women and children.

"Abu Nabeel has returned from his trip. He returned from N'York. Let's welcome him back."

They would come and sit in circles. The coffee tray would be passed around, then the tray of sweets. Um Nabeel would think of everything, including a large copper basin which she would fill with candies and unshelled peanuts to give to the children.

This had been the custom of Jurat Al-Sindyan for decades. Um Nabeel observed rituals and customs, and would let no occasion pass.

133

His mind was distracted. He saw himself there, and he saw himself here.

Now he was here and Raji was welcoming them at the door, standing between two women. One was fair and slim, and she smiled with reserve. This was Maggie, his wife. Radwan recognized her from pictures he had seen. The other had a darker complexion and a crown of whitish hair topped her head. This was Almas, Um Nabeel's sister. Her mother used to describe her: "Her hair was like cotton fluff." But the mother never took pleasure in what he was seeing. If he were to see this cotton fluff on hundreds of women, he would recognize her for she had similar features to the dearest face he had ever known.

The three of them came down the steps to the garden. The hugs began, tears fell and voices were hushed. It was as though time had stopped above the gateway to witness this historic moment.

Raji was the first to wake up from this distraction. He collected himself together, found his voice and said, "Please come in, everyone. Let's continue the greetings inside."

They all walked in silence among the garden trees that seemed to be clad in colorful autumn leaves just for the occasion.

Radwan turned but couldn't see the city.

He had lost New York in the dense trees of this garden.

Was he in New York?

Where was New York?

He continued walking with the group. The doors were opened in front of him and he entered a magnificent house that resembled a king's palace. He was afraid to tread on the elegant carpets. His feet instinctively stirred to be rid of his shoes at the threshold. But he abandoned the idea and decided to do what his hosts did.

He noticed that Raji's wife was not as young as she appeared in her picture that hung in the place of honor in his home. But she was the picture of liveliness and vitality. She climbed the stairs with agility and asked Lamya to follow her to the rooms she had prepared for her and her parents.

Um Nabeel excused herself because she could not climb the stairs. "Let me rest a while first."

Her legs had grown tired from standing. They often became weak with tremors that began in her eyes, then spread to her veins and reached her fingertips. She sat with her sister, her brother and her husband in the sitting room enjoying a reunion she had never dared to imagine, even in her dreams.

Their eyes were speaking in images and colors, even though their mouths were closed, the unexpected occasion robbing them of speech.

Almas was the first to break the silence. "O my sister, Raya, this is the reunion of my lifetime. You have changed much, but so have I and so has Raji. And the days have changed too."

Raji watched his two sisters hugging each other, contemplating their joy and reaching into the depths of these happy moments.

He was afraid to open his mouth in case he started to cry. He did not believe his eyes. He did not believe that his little sister had crossed the seven seas and come to visit him.

Radwan lit a cigarette and was content to listen.

134

One month had passed since Raji visited Canada. During this time, his life had changed visibly. The trip had rekindled a new spirit which had been smothered by the grey days of estrangement. He was once more in touch with things that he thought had been forever cut off.

He had felt this separation in various stages. It began when he pulled his feet out from the soil of his village and plunged them into this strange world. It then continued when he lost his father. But the shock which finally cut the last thread came with the death of his mother.

To him, his mother meant the earth and everything in it. It also meant the permanent promise of return. In his heart he returned to her every moment. But his busy days were against him, piling up and overcoming him.

He used to think that future days would give him the opportunity and that life would wait. But he learned too late that one should not wait for opportunities, but must create them, define their limits and steal them from the piles of preoccupations and responsibilities.

He learned, but it was too late. He now found one end of the old thread in his fingers, so he held on to it, clung to it with all his might.

His wife came to witness his newfound happiness. They were sitting around the table for supper.

"Raya, my dearest," Maggie said, "you've brought magic, you and Abu Nabeel. What is this secret which you both carried with you from the homeland?"

Um Nabeel answered, "It is the scent of the homeland."

"The scent of the homeland is enchanting, indeed. You're right, Um Nabeel. When I left the homeland, I was only six years old. Yet every moment here, I return to the scenes of my childhood. In my imagination, in my heart, in my dreams. I'm forever hanging by the thread of memories. I don't know whether I'll ever return."

Radwan interrupted.

"God willing, you will return, Um Raymond. Hopefully you will all return."

"Believe me when I tell you that Raji has started singing again. We've lived together for years but I've never heard him sing in Arabic."

"And it's old singing, too," Almas added. "Let's hear some, brother. Sing us some songs."

Raji's eyes began to smile and the smile spread over all his features. Maggie began to hum softly. He then hummed along with her as she sang.

> Love has brought me sorrow,
> Love, the source of my heart's grief.
> My days consumed, my nights turned to ashes
> By the fierce fires of love.
> O my dear, wise friends,
> If you could know my suffering
> You would weep for my despair,
> Though tears will not cure me.

"You have a great voice, Um Raymond!" Radwan applauded loudly as he asked her for more.

"These are very old songs," Raji apologized. "Perhaps they've been forgotten in the homeland."

Um Nabeel responded with excitement. "Our generation has not forgotten them, dear brother."

"Sing us another song," Almas begged. "'Speak to me by telephone only once' or 'Take me to my homeland by plane.'"

"Instead of asking others, why don't you do it yourself," Raji suggested cheerfully. "Let's hear you sing!"

Almas sighed. "Me? Alas, I have neither voice nor tune."

"We'll listen to a song by our brother-in-law, Abu Nabeel," Maggie prompted. "Surely his voice is wonderful."

Um Nabeel corrected her. "Abu Nabeel is good at dancing—much better than singing!"

"Great!" Maggie cried excitedly. "After supper, we'll turn the evening over to dancing!"

"There are still days ahead of us," Radwan protested.

"Our brother-in-law applies the Arabic proverb that says, 'Don't ask a singer to sing or a dancer to dance,'" Almas laughed.

"Abu Nabeel is tired," Raji defended him. "We'll excuse him tonight, on condition he promises to dance next time."

"God willing, dear Abu Raymond. May you remain ever well."

135

When you enter people's homes, you enter their hearts. You stretch out your hand, shaking the one stretched out to you. Eyes meet and you exchange smiles. Words dance out the tunes of conversation. The stranger then becomes a stranger once more. Each person withdraws to his inner self where he finds comfort, similar to the comfort of his own familiar bed after several sleepless nights elsewhere.

136

Radwan entered the house of his relatives, got acquainted with them and enjoyed their hospitality. He then slept on a comfortable bed, as soft as ostrich feathers, in a temperature-controlled room that protected him from the fluctuations of the weather. Um Nabeel plunged into this luxury with a sense of tranquillity and bliss, as if this visit had come in response to the hundreds of questions she had asked over the years.

Radwan, on the other hand, never stopped asking questions. He posed them to himself first. He was now thinking that, no matter how close he came to these people, a certain distance would continue to separate them. Those very moments, in fact, took him back to a feeling he had tried to get rid of long ago, to bury it under the ruins of years.

The question had gnawed away at him, making his heart bleed. Every time he heard someone in Jurat Al-Sindyan call him a stranger behind his back, he knew a stranger always remained a stranger. In villages one tries to cross the threshold, to enter and find oneself a seat with those who came before. But some invisible hand kept turning him away, pulling the seat out from under him.

Radwan remained an in-law, in spite of continual attempts to deepen the hole in which he planted his roots. For the land was not his land, the soil was not his soil, and his roots always felt that a layer of cold spread over them and separated them from the warmth of the deep earth.

From the first step he took inside Raji's garden, these feelings kept pulling at him: he loved Raji and admired him as a self-made man who had stood up to life with his defiant bare arms. He had stood up to it with an iron will which motivated him to establish a life in this alien land. He built this magnificent house, brought up a happy family and established a chain of stores that made his name famous in the new world.

Radwan came closer to Raji, trying to build a strong relationship that would compensate for the lost years. But he soon withdrew, and returned to his inner self which had become used to this kind of defeat.

When everybody had turned to chatting and singing on the previous evening, Radwan remained silent and deep in thought. He either listened to what was going on around him or let his imagination run away. He was a prey to strange ideas and notions. He wished to himself, if just one of his siblings would show up so that the scale would be balanced, raising his side to equal that of Um Nabeel, he would then face her relatives proudly and say, "Let me introduce you to my brother" or "to my brothers and sister."

He remembered a quotation he once heard from the parish priest at Jurat Al-Sindyan regarding the prodigal son. He repeated it in the silence deep within him: "This brother of yours was dead and has come back to life. He was lost and now he is found." How in the world was his brother to be found?

He felt the problem cling to him like thorns of a raspberry bush. This trip would be his only opportunity to find his siblings. How could he let this chance of a lifetime slip through his fingers?

137

He joined the others for breakfast while he was struggling with these thoughts and questions. He drank the American coffee with pleasure.

Raji's home was not like Nabeel's. Here the kitchen was American: there was no coffee flavored with cardamom, no tabbouli salad, no kibbi.

This was New York. Raji sipped the last of his coffee standing up. He had no time to finish his breakfast. He had to go early enough to catch the train and be on time for work. Only sickness kept him away; it would break the stern discipline which he always followed meticulously. He did not change his pace, even though he had reached the eighth decade of his life.

After her husband left, Maggie commented, half in jest, "Work is his first love." She did not continue but let the listeners understand that she came second. Yet she loved him and understood him well. She admired his strong will.

She asked her sister-in-law about the people of the homeland and whether they were all hard-working giants like her husband.

Then she added, as though talking to herself, "In fact, most of them are like that. I've seen them here, in this country." Her voice grew stronger as she continued. "They're all like him, battering against rocks and yet still going strong. It's with the arms of pioneers like him that America has been built up. They've laid down the foundations of progress. Some of them achieved success and their fingers touched the clouds, but many fell along the way. Competition is fierce and life is difficult. America belongs to the clever ones, as my mother used to say. Raji fell down twice in his difficult journey: once when his first store burned down, and once when a flood ruined his second store. But he was at the beginning of his career! This made him double his efforts and devote himself completely to his work. He would work and never stop to take a breath or to rest. When we met, he was living in a whirlwind. We loved each other but he gave me very little of his time. I thought, love can't be separated from sacrifice. If I wanted to be in his life, I had to give him a hand, to help him rather than take him away from his work. And so we lived happily together.

"When our children grew up, they refused to accept his way of life. In spite of respect and love for their father, they did not want to participate in any part of his business. They chose different kinds of jobs that left them time to enjoy their hobbies: sports, travel and the arts. This is what Raji cannot understand or accept. And it pains me, because I always hoped that the relationship between a father and his children would remain perfect and ideal. But I wonder if there is ever such a relationship. Their rebellion is part of their growth and independence. At any rate, thank God they're all good and loving children."

Maggie stopped talking. Besieged by silence, the echo of her words rebounded back to her. The group had listened without comment as she had unintentionally drawn a map for Raji's sister—a map of his endeavors since he first set foot in the New World.

138

Radwan listened with more interest than the others and one equation became clear to him: the stranger always remains a stranger, "the children of this country belong to this country."

This was what Nabeeha had said to him upon his arrival in Canada. He now understood why Raji plunged into his work. Work for Raji and other immigrants was an escape that helped them forget their alienation, their loneliness and their loss.

"The children of this country belong to this country."

Almas lived alone after she had planted her children in several cities.

"Each one of them is in a different city, honey. Yes, dear sister, each of my children lives in a different state. Distances between them are great. Sometimes it takes four hours by plane to get from one state to the other. All of them have their families and responsibilities. Yes, honey, they do come to visit me once a year. We try to make our meetings family reunions so that the grandchildren may get to know each other and the children might maintain a strong bond between them."

Radwan wondered, if Almas had been living alone for years, why had she not traveled even once to the homeland? Why did she not return to see her mother?

But he refrained from asking lest he should hurt her feelings. Perhaps the woman has a reason, man. Besides, why should you interfere in the private affairs of others? And don't forget how Almas came to America. You know the story. It had not been her decision. But in spite of that, her marriage to Mansoor Abu Absi was successful. She turned out to be a capable woman who shouldered the responsibility with courage. She bore her husband's children, brought up his children from a previous marriage and was to them as loving as any mother could be. Immigrants tell wonderful stories about her. Only Almas knows how much she sacrificed. Only she understands the little secrets concealed in the hidden places of the heart. Keep silent, man, keep your questions to yourself and just listen. It is better for you to remain a listener.

139

Maggie once again took the lead in the conversation.

"We've chosen today for you to visit the city. More correctly, to visit part of the city. New York is huge. If a person lived here his whole life, it would still be impossible to see everything."

"I'll go with you as long as we don't have to walk," Um Nabeel said.

"We'll take the car. Afterwards, we'll take the subway, that is, the underground train."

Um Nabeel became apprehensive. "I'll go with you when you go out for rides in the car. Today, why don't you just take Abu Nabeel and Lamya?"

Lamya knew New York from previous visits. But as long as her mother was happy staying here with Almas, she thought she might as well accompany her father and her uncle's wife.

Maggie drove the car confidently.

From the residential area she headed toward the city. New York soon loomed as a forest of gigantic buildings that touched the sky. As though in defense against the upward attack from earth, the sky sent down layers of dark grey fog.

Maggie left her car in a parking lot and walked with her two companions.

"It's just a short way to the subway station."

Radwan did not object. He let his companion take charge, expert as she was in roads and intersections, in the city above ground and below. "We're at your command, Um Raymond."

At her direction, they turned right and, within moments, entered a station. Soon afterwards they found themselves at the entrance of a tube which swallowed them along with hundreds of other people.

Radwan moved from the street to this tube, from the solid ground to moving electric stairs stretched out like the arms of a genie. They carried him downwards, with jostling crowds that resembled the crowds on the Day of Resurrection. From where he stood, he could see hundreds of heads and faces. Some people walked in his direction, others in the opposite direction, and the electric stairs sifted them and scattered them indifferently. The people entered and left in complete surrender, showing none of the signs that appeared on his forehead, his eyes and his lips. What was waiting for him in the underworld ? What were these crowds doing underground ?

He asked the question as if he was talking to himself.

"This is the fastest means of transport, Abu Nabeel," Maggie answered. "Down here there are no cars and no traffic jams, you'll see." He saw and did not believe. When he was on the train, he did not dare look outside. The train went as fast as a rocket, and he had to focus his eyes forward so he would not become dizzy and lose his balance.

He committed himself to his Creator and his two guardian angels, Maggie and Lamya.

"Do you like traveling on the train, Father?" Lamya asked in order to distract him, break the silence and bring him out of his isolation.

Radwan nodded. "It's a civilized, well-populated country, my dear daughter. No one can say otherwise. It's the land of wonders."

Lamya seized the opportunity. "Does this mean you'd like to stay here, you and my mother? We're ready to offer any help you might need. We'll take you out every day to see new places."

He was taken aback as though her words were electric currents.

"This country is beautiful, daughter, very beautiful....But its beauty belongs to its people. As for us, we have our country, our little village, which has a beauty of its own. We've become accustomed to living there."

"You can get accustomed to life here, in New York or in Canada," Maggie interjected. "Life here is easier than life in the village. Your children would be all around you, too."

Lamya and Maggie had cornered him, each one pressing a little bit further. He felt the noose getting tighter around his neck. He pulled himself free.

"May God preserve this country for its people. Um Raymond, I think old people like me would find it difficult to change our lifestyles. In our village, in Jurat Al-Sindyan, olive trees are planted when they are just little saplings. After they're planted and grown, and after they've lived twenty or fifty years, it becomes impossible to uproot them. If they're uprooted, they cannot live in soil other than their own. Um Nabeel and I are like those olive trees."

But his words did not convince Maggie. "Here, in America, they've developed new agricultural methods which make it possible to uproot trees and plant them again anywhere, whatever their age is."

Radwan was intrigued by this idea. But he said, "Tell me, Um Raymond. Have the agricultural experts in America ever tried to transplant some ancient oak or olive trees that are a thousand years old? I mean, anything like the oak trees and olive trees of Jurat Al-Sindyan?"

Maggie answered without waiting to consider what the old man meant. "All trees, Abu Nabeel... All trees are capable of being uprooted and planted again."

140

Radwan remained silent but unconvinced. He did not want to discuss with this good-hearted woman matters that he had experienced all his life. They had become part of his being like his very thoughts and blood. He did not want to say to her, the trees of your country are different, Um Raymond. In our country, olive trees as well as oak trees refuse to live in a soil other than their own.

He was now in New York. He had come to visit the city, and he was still on a train under its surface. He thought to himself, how could that ceiling above his head be strong enough to carry the city? Were there invisible props supporting it?

In the same manner as he had given up analyzing such complex matters when he first flew by airplane, he now saw it was better for him to stop thinking and just let the merciful hands guide him in these mysterious tunnels. A soft hand touched his to lead him off the train.

"We get off here, Father This is the last station We've arrived."

The three of them left the train and headed for the escalator that would carry them to one of the largest streets in the city.

Radwan stopped on the sidewalk, contemplating the scene. This was the first time he had touched down in the heart of the city, and his eyes climbed up the buildings. Maggie took it upon herself to be their tourist guide.

"This is the Woolworth Building. It's one of the oldest skyscrapers, Abu Nabeel. There are higher buildings now. Man's ambition is limitless."

He answered her while still gazing upwards. "Yet, Um Raymond, the Arabic proverb says, 'No tree has ever stretched up to its Creator'"

Maggie smiled in agreement. "You're right, Abu Nabeel, but modern man tries. He tries to transcend those trees. You know how many people have already traveled to the moon and tried to touch the stars? And men still continue their trips in that direction."

At a signal from Maggie, they stopped at the entrance to one of the skyscrapers.

Maggie pointed to the large elevator. "From under the ground, we'll now climb upwards to heaven."

"You're capable of doing that, Um Raymond?" Radwan teased. "At any rate, the company of good people like you can only lead to seventh heaven?"

"That's more than I deserve, Abu Nabeel!" Maggie said. "I meant the sky of New York only...Now let's go!"

141

The three of them entered the elevator along with many others. There were crowds everywhere in the city, always on the move in every direction. When he looked at them he did not know whether they were coming in or going out. They were constantly in motion as though it was their fate to remain that way forever.

The elevator was crowded with all sorts of people. Everyone kept silent and stared straight ahead. The elevator rose on its routine trip and stopped at the various floors. Theirs was number ninety.

Maggie invited him to get off and Lamya followed. The tourist guide's voice continued. "We'll cast a look at New York from above. What do you think, Abu Nabeel?"

What a question! Did he have words to obey his tongue? She raised him to the ninetieth floor above the ground and then asked, "What do you think?"

From the observation floor he looked out on a large section of the city. He stood still, his lips parted in wonder and amazement.

His eyes had never seen such scenes, nor his ears ever heard such noise. His eyes were dazed and his ears filled with a hum. He was afraid he was under a magic spell. Only the power of magic could have built such high buildings—a challenge to the Creator. It was almost sinful.

The hum in his ears became louder, disturbing him. He whispered to his daughter, "I hear a hum in my ears, daughter. What do you think it is?"

"I hear the same hum, Father," she reassured him. "This is natural and happens when one rises to a high place at great speed."

Happy with her explanation, he exclaimed, "And what a speed it was! The elevator rose like a rocket! You're right, Lamya, you're right."

"Take this chewing gum, Father. Chew it. It helps in such conditions."

"Chewing gum? Do you want me to chew gum at my age?"

Maggie interjected. "Take it and we'll do the same, Abu Nabeel. This chewing gum is like medicine!"

142

He felt the hum in his ears gradually disappear. In its place he began to hear words which were separate at first, then started to come together in harmonious composition until they finally became meaningful. He heard their echoes across the distance, across the years, on the tongue of an old priest.

"And the devil took Him up to a very high mountain and displayed before Him the world in all its magnificence, promising, 'All this will I bestow upon you if you kneel down in homage before me.' At this Jesus said to him, 'Away with thou. For it is written, Worship the Lord thy God and serve only Him.'"

Radwan stretched out his hands in protection from the glare of the city and from the temptations rising everywhere, pulling him toward the world and its glory. He took two steps back and closed his eyes.

"No, no. Go away, Satan. There is only one God I worship, one village I love, one home that waits for me on the other side of the sea."

All of a sudden he felt he had enough. He had had his fill of sightseeing: of buildings, gardens, streets, suspension bridges and truss bridges. He was now ready to withdraw...to return.

His daughter came closer to take a picture. Maggie put her arm around Radwan and smiled. Then she took one of Radwan and Lamya together.

The excursion had ended in success. The picture — the evidence — would stay with him. He would carry it back to the homeland and show it to every Thomas who doubted his stories about the wonders of this world and its miracles. He would place the picture in front of the man and say, "Here, see for yourself, my friend. Look. A picture is worth a thousand words."

143

Hasan the Clever tried to get through the city wall but a mighty giant stopped him.

"Strangers are forbidden to enter."

Hasan the Clever said, "I'm coming to look for my brother. He came to your city with a caravan of merchants and has not come back home."

The giant asked, "How many years ago did your brother enter our city?"

Hasan the Clever immediately answered, "He entered it on the day the silk market opened "

The giant roared and said mockingly, "Haven't you remembered to search for him since the silk market opened?"

Hasan the Clever said regretfully, "I was a little boy and my mother used to tell me, 'When you grow up, you will travel around to look for your brother.' But before I grew up, my mother died without telling me the way."

The giant asked, "And has your mother given you the distinguishing mark of your brother?"

"Yes." She said, 'Your brother has a mole under his right ear as big as a burnt coffee bean, and he has a birthmark in the shape of a mulberry on his left shoulder.'"

The giant nodded his head. "A mole, a distinguishing mark! And you say he entered the city when the silk market opened? Enter, enter, young man. The gates arc open before you. But don't forget that you have to leave the city before the fall of night."

144

Radwan entered the city, but the giant did not see him. He entered the magical gate carried on the wings of two angels, Maggie and Lamya, who walked beside him on sidewalks crowded with people.

He was dazed by faces of all colors and shapes. Some eyes looked at him and some did not, some rested on his face and did not speak. But all passed by him and in front of him as though they were moving statues. People moved quickly, and when they slowed down a little, they were pushed by the crowds, and almost thrown down.

Lamya's voice came to him from time to time, pointing out shop windows decorated with all kinds of desirable merchandise: clothes, house tools, strange instruments... He would withdraw his sight from the shop windows as though he were pushing away all temptations, all that might delay or distract him from his purpose, which was growing stronger with every step. He would look again at the faces with anguished eyes, searching for a face he had lost before the silk market opened.

The market had branched out now — it had become several markets with interconnected entrances and exits. In each market there were thousands of people moving as though they were an endlessly flowing fountain. The market pumped the streams and the tributaries all over the city, in the underground stations, in the elevators traveling between heaven and earth. In spite of that, the eyes remained vacant, and they never met. Radwan knew the Arabic folk saying: "A mountain will never meet another mountain, yet an eye will meet another eye." He wondered, where were the eyes he had searched for until he was exhausted?

Would a miracle happen? Would it appear like the light of a heavenly lamp to illuminate the empty darkness which overwhelmed him?

He heard Lamya say, "We'll enter through here, Father."

Her hand pointed to the entrance of a store. He obeyed his daughter, walking behind her, dragging his feet. Maggie had disappeared. The crowd had swallowed her.

"Where do all these people come from?"

He asked his question to the air. Lamya, always alert to him, answered, "We're in one of the world's largest cities, Father. Eight million people live in this city."

He nodded in understanding. "Yes, daughter, you're right. People in this country are like the sand of the sea. And yet I used to think Beirut was a large city. Poor Beirut."

These words came out spontaneously, and continued to echo in his consciousness long afterward.

Beirut was really poor, especially Beirut of the present. People traveled through it in order to escape, to get on board an airplane or a steamship. In days gone by, Beirut was a goddess of beauty, a mother of shops, a focus of all eyes and a stopping place for all travelers. When he left, it was wearing a mask of sadness and anguish.

He and Lamya stopped in front of a window where children's clothes were displayed.

"What do you think, Father? Wouldn't this dress be beautiful on Suzy?

He smiled as if he was seeing his granddaughter wearing the dress cut in the shape of a butterfly.

"It's very beautiful, daughter. Whatever Suzy wears suits her."

Lamya asked the saleswoman to wrap up the dress. The woman brought a box and another dress exactly the same so she wouldn't have to take the one out of the display. Radwan watched and was disturbed that there was another dress just like his granddaughter's. He asked Lamya why she accepted a dress other than the one she had chosen. Lamya reassured him that this was normal and that large stores had hundreds of the same dress.

Radwan thought, there were hundreds of each dress or raincoat, and there were millions of each face he saw. In spite of that, some faces remained distinct to him and conveyed special signs. They beckoned to him, they aroused tenderness in his heart, they caused tears of love to well up in this eves.

Radwan raised his head a little and saw Maggie waving excitedly to her two companions from a far corner, urging them over.

"Abu Nabeel, quick! Come and look, you and Lamya!"

A gigantic shop window was showing the latest electric inventions. A saleswoman pressed a button and a door opened. From the ceiling, tables and magnificent chairs descended.

In a moment the empty shop window was transformed into a reception room. With the descent of each piece of furniture, music played an accompanying tune.

The woman pressed another button and a hole opened in the ceiling. Beautiful young women descended wearing elegant dresses. They were coming to the imaginary reception and each of them gracefully selected a seat.

The saleswoman pressed another button and this time the ground split open and a young lady rose up as beautiful as the morning sunshine. Smiling and blowing kisses to no one in particular, she walked with coquettish steps close to Radwan. He looked and did not believe: was she a human or a genie? Her golden hair framed her face and flowed about her shoulders. Her slender body moved like a gazelle, her crimson lips parted like the Gate of Paradise, attainable only in dreams.

The young woman was walking toward him. He was afraid she would collide with him so he took a step backwards. He could not go back any further because of the dense crowd. He was afraid that this charming beauty would choose to address him with a word or a gesture that he would not understand. So he pretended he was looking through her into the distance. She passed by him and did not distinguish him from the others. She continued to pass out her neutral smiles and blow kisses to all, while admiring eyes surrounded her.

She then stopped at a window displaying a new detergent. She stood in the center, raised the detergent box and with graceful movements held it up for the crowd to see. Her lips then opened and closed uttering one single word, the commercial name of the commodity displayed for sale.

146

Radwan did not understand what was happening and thought the young woman was going to give the crowd presents. Lamya explained.

"This is only an attractive means of advertising, Father."

"And what are they advertising, daughter?"

She smiled. "A new detergent."

"Is it worth all the fuss? A beautiful blonde as bright as day, coming out of a magic box just like in the stories of *A Thousand and One Nights* to advertise a box of detergent?"

Lamya shrugged. "This is their way of selling things here."

He nodded in surrender. "I understand now, my daughter, I understand. I saw this scene on television, but I did not believe it. I thought it was some trick they had played. I have never thought that man's mind would be so trivial and that a young woman of flesh and blood would be happy to be such a showpiece."

"The young woman attracts attention, and this increases the amount of sales," Lamya explained.

"You're right, my daughter. But this is immoral, unethical. If I could speak to this beautiful young woman, I would say to her, 'This is unbecoming of you, my dear. You are a respectable, dignified and beautiful woman. Find yourself a more important job.'"

"This is her job, Father," Lamya laughed. "The woman gets a lot of money for this."

"That's not the point, my daughter. Whether she gets a lot or a little, that doesn't matter. What I will never understand is the relevance of this beautiful, sweet young woman to a handful of detergent!"

147

There were many other matters Radwan could not understand as he moved around in the large store in the big city. Rut he refrained from commenting. Dragging his tired feet, he left the store with his two companions. He became exhausted as he moved towards the end of the day, and he lost his earlier feeling of expectation and scattered dreams. No longer did that anticipation, suspended in his eyes, urge and goad him on like a spur, to walk briskly and shed the burden of old age.

148

They were on their way back. The city had received him and opened up its inner and outer gates. He had penetrated the city, from its deepest roots to its highest peaks. He got to know its people, its stores, its hustle and bustle, the narrowness of its wide avenues which only a stranger in a strange city could perceive. It kicked him in the head, reminding him at every step that there was no place for him here, not even a resting place for a goat or a bird's shadow.

When he first saw the city, he was attracted by an eagerness beyond his consciousness and his will, an eagerness that was present at every turn and every wink of the eye. He did not stop searching for them for a single moment.

Yes. He had asked the faces of strangers about them. He asked the streets and the buildings But he did not receive an answer.

His condition reminded him of stories he knew from his childhood about Hasan the Clever. Adults used to tell little ones such stories to help them through times of crisis and boredom. The stories held a special flavor, particularly on long desolate evenings when stormy weather and snow left them isolated, near a fireplace with a few oak logs and a dish of dried figs, raisins and nuts.

149

Hasan the Clever crossed the city from east to west. He passed by the giant's doorway and did not find the silk market. The markets opened then closed, moving him from entrance to exit, and in his own language he asked the people about his brother who had come to the city on the day the silk market opened. But the people passed by and did not understand his question. Not one of them volunteered to tell him that the language had changed since those days and there was no longer anyone who remembered a single word of it. Hasan the Clever refused to believe them and would not accept defeat.

He saw an old woman sitting on a street corner. He said to himself, this old woman may still know the language. Perhaps she's been here since the day the silk market opened.

He approached her with hesitant steps and saluted her. She looked at him and did not answer. Hasan the Clever repeated his greeting. "Peace be unto you, venerable lady."

He waited in silence.

Her lips opened and he expected she would give him the traditional answer which old women in his adventure stories gave: "If your greeting of peace had not preceded your conversation, I would have removed the flesh from your bones."

He wished she would say even this to him and start the conversation. But she remained wrapped up in silence and did not stir.

Hasan the Clever repeated, "Peace be unto you, O statue..."

She did not move. Statues never moved. He had turned around when he heard a voice whispering to him, "Wait, young man, wait."

He turned quickly but could no longer see the statue. The old woman had disappeared and in her place stood a young blonde woman wearing a crimson dress. He exclaimed in astonishment, "You? Who are you?"

"I am an unfortunate girl who was chosen to be guard of this city. They've frozen me into a statue."

"But you are an extremely beautiful young woman."

"This only happens when my lord and master is in a good mood," she said. "You have been fortunate to witness this event."

He did not believe what he was hearing. "Do you mean you'll be transformed back into an old woman?"

"Into a statue of an old woman."

He came closer to beg her, "Please, help me before you freeze again."

"What can I do for you?"

"Tell me, where does my brother live? My elder brother came to this city on the day the silk market opened and he has not yet returned home."

The woman roared with laughter. He heard the echoes all around him, bouncing on the open streets and exploding like crashes of thunder shaking the earth.

Hasan the Clever was afraid and no longer knew what to say or do. He had not said a single word that should cause this laughter. Why was the young woman laughing?

He turned around so he could apologize for any unintended error on his part. But the young woman had vanished, had dissolved like a grain of salt in water. In her place he saw a stone statue of an old woman.

He looked again, then began to run. He continued until he fell down unconscious.

150

Radwan touched his knees where he felt sharp pains. But he felt greater pain in his chest and between his ribs.

He had seen New York in the underground passages and on the ground above, where people flowed like waves in a stormy sea. He had seen it from great height when he had ridden the elevator with Maggie and Lamya to an observation deck next to heaven, where he had overcome all temptations.

He was now returning to his host's home, like a bird returning to its nest.   However long his trip might have been, and however far it might have taken him, he had to return to his life's companion.

In his absence, Um Nabeel had journeyed with her sister Almas across half a century, and had spoken all the unsaid words and stories stored in her memory. She had also heard all that Almas wanted to tell her about her own life in the new world. When Radwan returned, she was waiting eagerly as though he had been absent for ages.

He conveyed to her the day's adventure.

"It has been one of the most memorable days of my life, Um Nabeel. What can I tell you, my wife? I only wish you had been with us. Um Raymond left no stone in N'York unturned."

"On the contrary, Um Nabeel," Maggie said, "if you were to stay with us for a whole year, we would still not be able to see all of N'York. Today, we only saw a small section."

Radwan said with sincerity, "Small, yes. But its effect was big... As far as I'm concerned, I've had my rightful share."

151

Radwan retained in his memory every detail about his days in New York as though they had been engraved in stone. He did not neglect the smallest activity or event, and collected everything in inner cells and passages that neither moths nor dampness could reach, so that he might have a precious store for evenings back home.

He appreciated being in a city that was the paragon of cities, offering its visitor all the wonders and surprises he could ever dream of.

Radwan had thought his visit would end in a day or two, but the days passed one after another. Between morning and evening every day, there was a sweet time of new surprises, as the city opened new windows on its impressive beauty.

This was all wonderful to him, but his joy would only be complete if he were to hear some news about the three loved ones who lived on in his heart.

He had not brought up this subject since he asked Raji about them in Canada. But their names kept the beat of his footsteps on the sidewalks of New York, his memory of them never left his mind and their image clung to the light in his eyes.

Meanwhile, Raji continued his search for them without Radwan's knowledge.

Since his return from Canada, his brother-in-law's question kept ringing in his ears, day after day.

"My dear Abu Raymond, have you heard anything about my brothers Saad and Yusef, and my sister Adla? They emigrated to N'York a long time ago before the 1914 war. They left and did not write. They emigrated and destroyed all bridges behind them. They cut off all ties and a heavy curtain descended between them and their past."

Was this what actually happened?

Or were things different?

Who could tell anything about them? Who could describe what happened to them and others in that dark period of the history of immigration? Who could tell?

He looked up old names in his telephone directory, persons he knew a long time ago, and he asked each of them the same question: "Do you know anything about the Abu Yusef siblings?"

He gave them his telephone number at the store so that if anyone called him the matter would remain his task alone. He didn't want his wife or his sister to know.

He received many calls, but the answers were negative. People in this city did not look back. Their eyes looked to the future...always to the future.

152

He had almost closed the doors on the whole business when he received an unusual phone call. Someone he did not know called to say he had information regarding Radwan's siblings. But he wouldn't leave his name.

"When we meet, we'll get acquainted, Mr. Raji..."

The man spoke with an American accent, but included broken Arabic words in his conversation. Although Raji was less than satisfied with the man's evasiveness, he agreed to see him nonetheless. They made an appointment to meet at the restaurant next to his store.

"We'll meet there at noon."

"Okay!, Mr. Raji. Agreed."

Raji remembered only after he hung up that they had not discussed how they would know one another. But he realized that this would not be a problem. The cafeteria was almost a closed club, frequented mainly by the employees and businessmen of the nearby stores and offices. New faces stood out.

He was right. As soon as he entered, he noticed a man sitting alone. He approached and greeted him.

"Good day. I am Raji Abu Nijim. And you are. . .?"

The man stood up and enthusiastically shook his hand.

"I am Theodore Noon. Please call me Ted. How are you, Mr. Nijim?"

"Fine.... Please come let's get our food and we'll talk over lunch."

153

Raji did not wait for the man to answer. They joined the end of the line of customers, tilled their trays and returned to the table.

Raji began the conversation. "Mr. Noon, do you live in New York?"

"Yes, yes, Mr. Nijim," the man answered nervously. "I used to work at a big store, Sprinkley Department Stores. You've heard of them? I'm retired now."

"Oh! You're originally from our homeland?"

"Yes, yes. We're from Umra."

"Perhaps the name was Qumra and has been changed," Raji interjected. "Did you emigrate a long time ago?"

"Yes, many years ago. My family came here when I was seven. Later I studied accounting and got a job. I'm a bachelor now, Mr. Nijim. I mean I'm not married. I used to be married, and I divorced my wife. She was American, and it didn't workout."

"Well, sometimes temperaments differ," Raji said. "The important thing in divorce is the children."

"No, no...thank God. There were no children."

Raji returned to the subject at hand. "Mr. Noon, regarding your telephone call, let's continue our conversation. What information do you have on the Abu Yusef siblings? They emigrated to New York before the First World War and there was no news of them after that."

"Yes, Mr. Nijim. I have news. It's a long story. Do you have time to listen?"

"Of course," Raji said, encouraging him. "That's why I'm here."

"I heard the story from my father, Sam Noon, God bless his soul. We immigrated at the same time and met the Abu Yusef siblings— that is Adele, Cyd and Joe—in Marseilles. From there, we traveled together on a steamship that brought us to the New York harbor. We stayed together for a longtime...a long time."

Suddenly Ted stopped. Raji's heart jumped into his throat.

"What's the matter, Mr. Noon? What happened?"

He smiled. "Nothing, nothing, Mr. Nijim. I've forgotten to take off my hat and coat."

"Please, make yourself at home."

154

The man put his overcoat and hat on a nearby chair and continued his story.

"When we arrived in New York, we had no friends and no address to go to. The police took us to a special center where immigrants were gathered. From there, we began to disperse. We stayed with the three siblings, and we found a room in which we lived together for several months. Everyday, the men went out looking for work. My mother and Adele stayed at home to prepare the meals—beans and canned food given to them by the Department of Immigration. One day Joe was lucky to find a job as a servant in the store of a Syrian merchant who paid him twenty cents a day. Everybody rejoiced and we celebrated the occasion, opening a can of meat in addition to the beans. Two days later my father found a job. A merchant gave him a backpack and asked him to sell his merchandise in the countryside. He was away from home for several days— sometimes ten, sometimes twenty—after which he'd return, tired but happy with the results. My mother began to save her money in her cummerbund... Do you know what a cummerbund is, Mr. Nijim?"

"Yes, yes, I know." Raji listened to the marginal details hoping for more important information: what happened to them? He was afraid their meeting would end before the man finished his introduction. So he urged him to continue.

"Cyd refused to carry a backpack and would not accept work for the poor wages at a merchant's store. Yes, Cyd was different. He was an amateur wrestler. His body was a piece of rock. This is what my father used to say about him.

"Cyd began looking for work among circles of wrestlers. He was fortunate to meet a Lebanese immigrant who ran a wrestling ring. He took him in and watched him wrestle. He liked Cyd and found him a trainer.

"One day, a strange thing happened. The state's wrestling champion came to the ring. Most of the wrestlers there were afraid to face him. Like us, he was an immigrant from the area of Jbail. My father told me that. The wrestler's professional name was Deek al-Jinn, 'the genie's rooster.'

"He entered the arena and began walking about, challenging with his swaggering gait and defiant looks, shouting loudly, 'Shore man...mountain man.' This meant that he was a shore man challenging those from the mountain. Cyd was a mountain man and could not bear to leave the challenge unmet, so he stood up and said, 'Say shore man only. Don't dare mention the name of the mountain!'

"Deek al-Jinn continued his challenge: 'Shore man...mountain man. I say it loud and clear.' So Cyd took off his shirt and invited him to wrestle. When the club owner saw what was happening, he leapt up behind Cyd and caught him by the arm. He tried to pull him away from the giant, who had much more experience and strength.

"Cyd did not listen to the words of the club owner. He pushed him aside and jumped into the arena. 'The mountain man is waiting here for you... come on.'

"The spectators were divided into two groups, one supporting Deek al-Jinn and the other applauding the unknown adventurer who was walking towards certain death. Deek al-Jinn took a giant leap into the arena and faced his fiery, angry opponent. The champion had hardly moved when Cyd handed him a powerful blow, knocking him down. When Deck al-Jinn tried to stand up, Cyd gave him another fast blow, his fingers piercing the champion's belly. The man fell down writhing in pain.

"The spectators were shocked. They did not clap or shout. They waited until the ambulance arrived and carried the giant wrestler to the nearest hospital where he underwent surgery that saved his life. As for Cyd, he was expelled from the club for disobeying the rules of wrestling.

"When he returned to the room that evening, he was sad and depressed. He talked to no one about what had happened. We learned the story later from other immigrants.

"After this, Cyd no longer mentioned wrestling. He stopped all sporting activities and turned his attention to looking for a job. Then he disappeared for a long time. We later found out from his brother Joe that he had joined a caravan heading west where he found work on a cattle ranch.

"After his departure, the group began to break up. Joe moved from one store to another until he ended up the partner of an old man who owned a restaurant in Boston. Adele got married to a young immigrant and moved to a state in the south. My father continued to peddle goods until he had enough money to open a small restaurant where my mother did what she was good at — cooking the meals. I used to help in the restaurant and go to school. I learned accounting and ended up in a respectable company."

Raji interrupted. "This is all old story, Mr. Noon. What happened after that? Do you have any information?"

Ted nodded his head. "Yes, yes. Joe kept in touch with my father and visited us on holidays. He used to give us news of his brother and sister. But when my father died, we no longer heard anything about them."

Raji asked, "And when did your father die, Mr. Noon?"

"After the First World War."

"And since that time, none of them has ever contacted you ?"

"Mr. Nijim, everyone is busy with his own affairs. The adults grow old and the children know nothing about us. This is the way it is."

Raji was in no mood for the man's philosophy. He felt this was all he could get out of him. But he posed on last question.

"Do you still have any of their addresses? Or do you know any-one who does?"

Ted shook his head. "No, no, Mr. Nijim. This is all I know. I've told you everything. I just wanted to help, you see...I must go now. It has been nice meeting you."

Raji shook hands with the man. "Nice meeting you, too, Mr. Noon. And thank you for the story."

The man answered cheerfully, "And thank you for the lunch. Good-bye."

Raji stood up, contemplated him for a while, then took his hat and walked out.

155

It was two o'clock.

He had spent two hours with the man. Why? Had this inter-view benefited him? Had he learned anything new that would make Radwan happy?

He reflected on all the man had told him as he walked this fa-miliar sidewalk. A fine drizzle wet his face and head because he had forgotten to put on the hat he held in his hand.   Thoughts rumbled around in his head and the questions mounted. Should he tell Radwan or should he not? Would it help him to know what went on today with the man from the past? What good would sto-ries over half a century old do? By the time he reached his store, he had made a decision: he would tell Radwan everything. It was nec-essary for him to know these distant stories. Maybe then he could get rid of the obsession that clung to him like his own shadow, and to stop thinking that his brothers and sister — or their children — were somewhere in New York.

He also decided to go even further than the stories he had heard. He would say, "My dear brother Radwan, your case is a repetition of thousands. Your brothers and sister are like many immigrants who came through this city when they first arrived. Then, they scat-tered all over the American continent, changed their names, their clothes and many of their ideas after several disappointments and failures. Perhaps most of them succeeded later on and became pros-perous and well-established. But all this would have happened to the new person in each of them, to the newborn who had risen from his own ashes...."

He would also say, "If they did not write, that does not mean that they had lost all their feelings. Perhaps it was because they had lost all hope. The war clouded their minds, shocked their souls and blinded their eyes. The war tore people apart and implanted a new alienation in the already alienated souls.

"How much can a human being suffer? How long can he remain on his feet, resisting and standing up to these odds?"

He would also tell him much more that would surely wipe out that distant and deep-seated sadness, and save him from the devils that tormented him.

Then Raji wondered, if he saved him from this anxiety, what would he give him in return?

Hope?

Yes, of course! That was what Radwan should carry back with him to the young ones. For they were his hope, as were his grandchildren—his gift to future generations, the extension of his own life in the unknown.

He would tell him much this evening when they met.

156

That evening Radwan was silent as if he were digesting the rich meal that New York had been for the last ten days. He was calm and exhausted. New York was boiling within him flowing through his blood stream, penetrating his very being.

If he stopped inquiring about his brothers and sister, that did not mean he had forgotten them but rather the question had become an echo that knocked but was never answered.

157

Surely there is someone who answers, my dear Radwan. There is someone who carries the burden along with you and tries to lighten it. He tries...Raji wondered.

Was he really trying? It was a risk, he thought to himself. But he was not afraid of risks. He was sorry to leave Radwan in suspense, ending his visit without hearing a word that would comfort him on his return journey.

So he began, right from the beginning.

"Radwan...."

"Yes, Abu Raymond. Yes, my dear brother."

Radwan was all eyes and ears. If Raji did not have something important on his mind, he would not address him so seriously.

"My dear Radwan. We have looked for your brothers and sister. In fact, I began looking as soon as I returned from Canada. All the answers were negative, until today."

"And what happened today, Abu Raymond?" he asked seriously. "I hope it was something good."

Raji was silent for a moment. Then he began. "Today, a man called me and said he had information. I invited him to lunch and we sat talking for two hours. He had much information. But it was over half a century old. He told me about the early years in detail. Then, when your brothers and sister separated, he lost track of them. His name, by the way, was Theodore Noon. Does this ring a bell?"

Radwan shook his head and Raji continued. "According to him, your brothers and sister went north, west and south. That is almost over all the states of America. None of them remained in New York. Alder's name became Adele, Yusef became Joe and Saad, Cyd. The man told me your brothers and sister were friends of his father, Sam Noon. When the father died after the First World War, nobody heard anything more about them.

"The story is no doubt a painful one, Abu Nabeel. I wish I could help you find even a clue. Alas, all my efforts have been in vain. We must be realistic, you know, and face the facts. May God preserve the young ones and bless their children."

Radwan nodded. "Thank God, Abu Raymond, I have everything. But there is no person who can really take the place of another. A son is loved in one way, and a brother in another. But I am ready to accept what you see fitting."

"I think you have beautiful days ahead to spend with your children and grandchildren, and to be happy in their company. Trust in God, He takes care of everyone."

"True," Radwan agreed. "God has taken care of them when the seven seas separated us. He alone will continue to take care of them. May God grant them happiness wherever they may be."

Radwan stressed this last sentence. He then got up, but was unable to straighten his back. He could not walk upright. The information had hit a bone in his spine, sending splinters into his heart. His eyes were bathed in tears. He went out on the porch to escape.

There was a slight autumn wind wandering in the garden, shaking the birds from the trees before wandering out to the neighboring gardens. He felt a sudden eagerness, not for his children, his grandchildren or his siblings...but for that good earth that stretched out its arms to enfold him whenever life dealt a blow that he could not take.

He took out his handkerchief and wiped his eyes slowly, then returned inside to join in the drinks, the food, the evening gathering and the conversation.

158

It was the farewell evening.

At dawn, the airplane would carry them back to Canada.

Maggie used the occasion to try to pull Radwan out of his shell.

"You didn't sing to us, Abu Nabeel. But we have not forgotten your promise to dance"

Maggie could have asked him anything but that. How could he dance after what Raji had just said? His back hurt and he felt the pain sinking into the marrow of his bones.

"One short little dance," Maggie insisted, "so that we may learn new steps from you."

He looked into her kind face and imploring eyes that resembled those of a child begging for a special birthday gift. He remembered everything she had done for him and his wife during their visit, how she had taken them all over the city and the suburbs, sometimes by car, sometimes on foot. Her smile had been a guiding hand opening all doors.

She was now giving him the same kind smile, asking nothing for herself, but for the whole group.

He felt his heart throb in a new way. A few hours from now he would be traveling. He would disappear from her sight, from Raji's, and from Almas', for an unknown period of time, perhaps forever. They wanted him to dance. Could he apologize and be excused just because he was tired and in low spirits?

Yet, dance expressed all kinds of moods — not only joy. There were dances for sorrow, for pain, for defeat and even for death.

He leapt up, tied a shawl around his hips and began dancing to the beat of clapping hands and the music from an old Arabic record.

He was dancing for them. He was getting out of his body and his pain, throwing himself into the group, becoming one with them. But he could not feel that old enthusiasm that usually coursed through his veins, electrifying him.

He tried to smile and, throughout his dancing, express his thanks and gratitude to those beloved ones he had discovered in this otherwise indifferent city. They compensated for his lost siblings. But his legs did not respond. He felt he was a defeated horse, the whip cracking above his head, goading him on to win the race. He pulled his legs up as though he was tearing them away from a strong magnet beneath the floorboards.

He spun around several times, then danced around the whole group. Finally he excused himself and returned to his seat amid applause and loud praises of admiration.

Even those cold steps which expressed his weariness and pain were meaningful to them. Or did they perceive his defeat and applaud, not out of admiration, but out of sheer politeness and encouragement? Even if the latter were true, what was the difference? What did it matter to him now if he danced or crept like an ant?

Nothing mattered anymore. Nothing. His anxiety had disappeared but his sorrow remained His curiosity vanished, leaving a great emptiness within him. He had put an end to the ardent eagerness in his chest that had made him move about in the strange city like a determined young man. He had walked tirelessly, descending into the depths of the earth and soaring among the clouds. He had done this without any feeling of weakness, hunger or bodily desire Only a burning emotion remained, hidden beneath the castles he had built in the air.

He had done all he could. Raji had also done his best. But disappointment was Radwan's lot. It showed in the heavy weary dance in which he had attempted to chase defeat and bitterness from his innermost being.

159

As though talking to herself, Almas said, "You will be traveling tomorrow, honey, and you will leave a big void in our life. We just got to know you and now you are going away. I can't believe it, I don't want to believe it."

She went on, "One may live fifty years away from one's sister or brother, honey. But after meeting again, separation becomes so difficult."

"It is also difficult for me, sister," Um Nabeel answered. "I wish I could stay with you all my life."

"Staying is easier than leaving," Raji said. "You are quite welcome here. That is all we wish for, sister, that you and Abu Nabeel live with us. You would get used to life in this country, especially since conditions back in the homeland don't encourage one to return. The number of casualties rises every day in Beirut and in the mountains. The area of fighting is expanding and Lebanon is now on the edge of a volcano. War there is always the first mentioned in newscasts, here and everywhere. This interest the media seems to have makes me suspicious."

Radwan interrupted. "We had noticed the change before we left. Barricades and road blocks were all over the streets of Beirut. But we never thought it would reach this stage."

"Yes, my dear Abu Nabeel," Raji answered. "The situation is quite critical. No one can estimate where this war will lead our little homeland."

"God have mercy and be kind to us," Um Nabeel murmured.

"Honey," Almas said, "conditions are bad and it is better for everyone that you stay with us or in Canada until things improve."

The dialogue reached Radwan's ears, increasing his pain and distress. But he decided to stay out of the discussion. In a few hours he would return to Canada and then he would talk it over with his children. He knew well what he would do, in spite of all the enticements. He would not announce his intention now. He would not say a word. Let them talk all they liked, but he had resolved there was only one idea, only one path to follow, whatever the price.

With these thoughts in mind, he slept. The next morning he finished packing, put his clothes on and prepared to leave.

160

Every step had a different echo in relation to previous ones, Radwan thought. Had he recorded all his emotions since his trip started, he would have had a chest close to bursting. He was now preparing to leave this wonderful city and the relatives who almost replaced his own. He felt the lump in his throat might choke him. He fought back tears so that he might not expose his weakness in front of the others.

Um Nabeel cried silently and passionately. Her burning emotions rose to her wet lashes and brushed the forehead of her brother who was bending over her shoulder. The self-made giant of a man, her brother, was also crying. He embraced her tightly and poured into her heart all his love for a land he had left in spite of himself, for a mother who had died in anguish at his absence, and for those distant days rooted with the oaks of his remote village.

Um Nabeel slipped out of his arms to embrace her sister. Almas dried her tears, and said, "My dear sister, my sweet one. I have not seen enough of you. How the days have passed us by!"

Maggie looked pensive and wiped her eyes. She knew that, in a short while, the dramatic scene would end and the silent hum of monotonous days would be hers again. Soon the unusual movement that had entered her life would calm down and matters would return to their normal flow. The airplane would carry the two guests back, as it had carried them to her a few days earlier and interrupted the silence and broken the hum drum of her life. At the same time, she was trying to hide the bite of jealousy she felt in her heart, seeing the arms of her husband embracing his sister and resting on her shoulders. To push away these disturbing thoughts, she turned toward Radwan and noticed a similar emotion in his eyes.

She approached him, held his hand and said, "They have been sweet memorable days, Abu Nabeel. Their taste will remain with us for a long time to come."

Maggie's words were the last arrow that tore into his heart, leaving a gaping wound. Radwan began to cry. He tried to say a few words but his lips were quivering. He was content with accepting the embrace of Maggie's soft arms. Quickly he said good-bye to Almas and Raji, and went off with Um Nabeel and Lamya towards the airport.

161

Charlottetown embraced them again. It appeared to Radwan a comfortable and familiar world. He even felt he was landing on intimate soil in which he had planted part of himself.   How great was the difference between the endless city which he had left and this small town receiving him! He had come to know a lot about it and, in a few days, he would know all its streets and houses by heart. In a few days

From now on, he would begin counting the days, even the hours and minutes The journey had reached its pinnacle. Returning to Charlottetown was a relapse and it did not have the flavor of enthusiasm as the first coming did.

He came down the stairs of the airplane, nursing these thoughts, to be received by loving arms once more. He forgot his distress, his pain and his disappointments. He forgot the isolation that fluttered around him on grey wings, then disappeared behind laughing eyes and pleasant faces which spread comfort and reassurance on his and his wife's path.

"Thank God for your safety."

"We missed you."

"Your absence in N'York was longer than all the past years."

"We waited eagerly for your return."

"How were we able to live so far from you all these years?"

His children welcomed him back, saying aloud what he was keeping inside, surging and beating at his ribs, knocking at the walls of his heart.

Radwan was not the same as when he had left them. Hassan noticed and whispered in Nabeel's ear, "My father is silent, contrary to his custom."

Nabeel answered, "Perhaps he is tired from traveling."

"I don't think it's that. We will soon know the whole story from Lamya."

Lamya had heard the story from her Uncle Raji. He advised her to take particular care of her father, whose disappointment was greater than expected.

Her uncle had said, "I don't blame him, Lamya. It is very difficult to forget one's brothers and sister, and be convinced that they are lost forever."

"Do you think my father is convinced?" Lamya had asked. "He seemed to be. But what he keeps inside is known only to God."

Lamya knew her father well and understood how difficult it was for others to make him change his mind about anything. By instinct, she felt that her father showed he was convinced out of politeness, but kept his disturbing thoughts to himself alone.

"But," Lamya asked herself again, "where can he now look for his brothers and sister?"

162

She later asked her brothers the same question when they took her aside to find out what had happened to their father.

"The subject will trouble him for some time but he will soon forget it in the busy activities of life here," Nabeel said.

Hassan added, "I believe that this is a good opportunity to broach the subject of his staying here. Besides, who knows? We may be able to find some trace of them one day."

Lamya expressed her reservations. "Do you want to know what I think? I believe my father is ready to go back home. . .now."

Hassan was shaken. "But it is war there. Conditions in the homeland are horrible. Don't you hear the news? There are dozens killed and wounded daily. People are being kidnapped because of their religion shown on their identity cards. It is an appalling situation."

Nabeel agreed. "We shall never allow them to return home, whatever it costs," he insisted. "We will not throw our parents into the jaws of hell!"

"That is your opinion, Nabeel," Lamya said calmly. "It is not our father's. Why don't you discuss the matter with him?"

Nabeel shook his head. "I already did, but our father cannot estimate the size of the catastrophe. He judges things emotionally and his emotion is tied up with that little spot of the world."

"Do you blame him, Nabeel?" Hassan asked. "Are you not like him, too? And me too? And Lamya? Aren't all our brothers and sisters? We are all tied to the womb that brought us into the world. Whatever land we own here, we will never feel that this earth is our earth."

"That is true, Hassan," Nabeel nodded. "But for the time being, we have to go against our feelings and against the natural flow of our ideas. Our concern now is to do everything within our power to save the lives of our parents. It is as simple as that. The matter cannot be put up for bargaining: it is a matter of life or death."

163

"She loves me, she loves me not... She loves me, she loves me not... She loves..."

"Yes, indeed, she loves you, my dear grandson."

The words froze on Michael's lips as his grandfather surprised him in the middle of his game. The paper daisy fell from his hand. He was alone in his room, humming children's songs and imitating his elder brothers by picking the white petals off the artificial flower, one for love and one for not. When his grandfather entered the room, the boy stopped playing.

Radwan approached him, begging, "Continue, grandson, continue your game. Teach me the words you are saying."

The boy smiled bashfully, bent over to pick up the flower and continued his game. "She loves me, she loves me not..."

Radwan took a similar flower and began imitating his grandson. Peace, war.... Peace, war... We return, we don't return... We return, we don't...return..."

164

He felt there was no alternative but to return as soon as possible. This had become his preoccupation since his return from New York. The homeland had become the only voice echoing in his soul. These were difficult and harsh days. Fire consumed the marketplaces of Beirut and the factories in the suburbs. This news scorched the eyes of emigrants with its heat, forcing tears into them.

It followed him across the seas and clung tightly to him. He found no place to hide. War was on everyone's lips wherever people met. Newscasts, newspapers, and, above all, television, conveyed to them the smallest details of the battles taking place: how sniping happened on the front lines; how innocent people fell in the streets; how citizens out on daily errands became casualties, one falling down with a loaf of bread in his hand, another dropping from a ladder he had climbed to reconnect an electric wire; how groups moved as fugitives in fear and apprehension; how blood was shed, wounds were inflicted and terror was reflected in everyone's eyes.

It was the war of the poor and the wretched.

Radwan said silently, "Theirs is the Kingdom of Heaven."

But was this how the Kingdom of Heaven was? People were fleeing barefoot, half-naked. They were escaping from the burning missiles and blazing fires. They were moving from one shelter to another carrying whatever they could on their heads and shoulders.

Here was a bomb exploding in a residential area, with human shreds flying in the air as photographers' lenses captured the event with amazing accuracy, sparing no detail. Television stations in Canada and the United States brought them the images. The little homeland was soon chaotically distributed on small screens everywhere. The announcer's voice rose with each new atrocity. What was he saying?

It did not concern Radwan to know. Pictures were more eloquent than words. The man's voice rose, pleading to all the world to witness the horror of what was happening. The lens passed over the skeletons of buildings that looked like skulls and bones from thousands of years ago.

Was this Beirut or were these archaeological ruins?

Nabeel explained. "This is Beirut, Father, this is Beirut. Can you believe what is happening there?"

The announcer's voice continued and bloody scenes followed: burnt bodies of children, human skeletons heaped on top of wooden huts or in open pits gaping like hungry mouths, houses falling down and survivors leaping out of them only to be gunned down by snipers' automatic guns from hidden corners, bulldozers sweeping away dirt and corpses. The announcer's voice went on and on.

165

He turned his eyes away from the television screen and began to shed tears of deep sorrow What was happening in his homeland?

Nabeel tried to explain. "From day to day, the ferocity of the fighting increases. Where is this going to lead?"

"His father asked, wishing that he did not have to know: "Who is fighting whom, Son?"

"The conflicting parties. That is what the news says."

"And who are those parties? From where have they gathered so much hatred and so many grudges that can destroy homes right over the heads of the people? What are they fighting for, my son?"

His son replied, "For the liberation of the homeland. This is what they claim."

Deep inside, Radwan wished he were there, to understand the story better and know what caused the disagreement.

Suddenly, he was overcome by a feeling he had never known before—a mixture of great fear, loneliness, weakness and almost paralysis.

If he could only wipe out this vast distance that separated him from his homeland. If he had wings he would have flown there this very instant without even telling his wife and children. Like a bird, he would carry drops of water to extinguish the fires. He would call out repeatedly to the fighters and then reconcile them, exactly as he used to do whenever there was a fight in Jurat Al-Sindyan.

How often fighting had broken out in his village! He would go out bravely to reconcile the enemies, or he would open his home to protect an escapee from the fires of conflict and the showers of stones coming from every direction.

And what were their weapons then? Stones, sticks and clubs...anything they could lay their hands on. The fighters were two groups, with a third group always remaining neutral to intervene at the right time and bring about a reconciliation. If peace were not possible because of heated emotions and fiery tempers, the matter was postponed a few days, until it could be raised with the elders of the village. Witnesses would be called, the wrongdoer would admit to his fault and either be forgiven or receive punishment. Cordial relations would be re-established and grudges would dissolve like soap bubbles. And Jurat Al-Sindyan would live peacefully until it was disturbed by another problem or a new aggression.

But what he was seeing now on the television screen had no name and was not like anything he knew. He turned around, looking for someone to listen to him, to hear his ideas. He saw Nabeel opposite him, his head in his hands and his eyes staring at the floor.

He did not say a word lest he disturb his son. He was more afraid that his voice would come out weeping. He left and went to the next room.

166

The family was gathered in the living room at Nabeel's invitation. The invitation was not limited to his siblings and in-laws but it included most of the Lebanese immigrants on the Island. The purpose of the meeting was to discuss the war in Lebanon and to invite everyone to donate funds to help those who were suffering.

No one turned down the invitation. Everyone was present at the appointed time. They came with enthusiasm and the place was crowded. Mu'een suggested they move to a larger hall more suitable for public meetings. But Nabeel objected to his brother-in-law's suggestion.

"We gathered here tonight, Mu'een, not to hold a formal meeting but only to discuss what action is necessary. Let us continue our dialogue here tonight, and hold future meetings at the hall."

The idea was accepted.

Shihadeh was the first to ask, "If it is at all possible, brothers, could you please clarify the purpose of this meeting for all of us?"

Addressing everyone, Nabeel said, "The people here have decided to help alleviate the pain of their fellow citizens in the homeland, especially those who have been directly afflicted by the war. We will collect contributions to help them."

Jibran interrupted. "That is a great idea, Nabeel. This will create a new enthusiasm in the club."

"And an untraditional activity," Nawal added. "We have been accustomed to evening parties and entertainment. That was fine in times of peace. Now there is something more important. There is a nation, our nation, our own flesh and blood, being exposed to death at every turn. Are we going to remain passive onlookers?"

Everyone responded: "Of course not. We are ready for anything."

As president of the club, Mu'een asked, "Shall we prepare for future meetings? When should we hold them?"

"I think we should hold the meetings every evening so that anyone who wants to help may do so," Nabeel suggested. "Whenever any of us finishes his work, he can drop in and offer whatever help or suggestions he can. I hope it is understood by everyone that we are doing this of our own accord, and are not prompted by any political affiliation back home. Our purpose is humanitarian."

Shihadeh applauded. "Well-said! We are all brethren and as brethren we shall work together."

"May God give you long life, Uncle Shihadeh. You are always the source of good deeds," Nabeel said, thanking him.

He had hardly finished this sentence when Sami Ghaddar stood up. Pausing for effect, he puffed out his chest.

Everyone was silent. They waited. They all knew Sami and his reputation for opposing everything. This was a golden opportunity to oppose the idea.

"Would you kindly clarify a number of points, Mr. Nabeel ?"

The tone of his voice was challenging and provoking. Nabeel refused to be challenged or provoked by anyone. He would not accept any suspicion placed upon him, especially when his purpose was as noble as the one he was calling for.

"What points, brother Sami?"

Sami answered without changing his tone of voice. "There are many obscure points. For example, you said that no party contacted you. This means that our help will not be identified with any political party."

Nabeel tried to answer him, but Mu'een jumped in. "Nabeel has described the nature of the action. In the first place, it is humanitarian."

Sami smiled sardonically. "Your answer is naive, brother Mu'een. With the present conditions, there is no longer any act that is absolutely humanitarian. You have to define your position vis-à-vis the fighting first, and determine whose side you are on and which party you sympathize with."

"Ho, ho!" Mu'een shouted angrily. "We are not in a battlefield to support one party against another. We are living the tragedy of our homeland with all its parties and sides. We shall not permit anyone to divide us."

He then addressed the group. "Is there anyone among you who objects to what I've said?"

When no one responded, he continued. "You are alone, brother Sami. You are the only person objecting to a humanitarian deed where we are trying to be unified, not divided."

Not a hair on Sami Ghaddar's head moved. He took a challenging step forward.

"There is no reason for me to be with you them. Our goals do not coincide."

"You are free," Nabeel answered. "So is everyone listening to me. There is no obligation for anyone to do anything. Each one of you is completely free to stay or go."

As he moved toward the door, Sami said, "I have defined my position. I repeat: I shall not help unless the identity of those benefiting from my help is clear. Good night, everyone."

Only Nabeel's voice accompanied him to the door. The group remained silent as though trying to recapture the harmonious ideas of before, when Sami had thrown his stone into the calm pool.

Jibran Abu Hamad was the first to break the silence. "Sami has to have some visible role to perform at every occasion."

Nabeel answered calmly. "Sami is free to think and behave as he likes."

"Of course he is free." Jibran spoke mockingly. But freedom differs according to people's interpretations. One may use his freedom to construct or to destroy."

"Sami's contradiction remains a tempest in a teacup," Nabeel reassured him. "What we actually accomplish here is the most important thing."

"We are all ready to serve, brother Nabeel." Jibran spoke for the whole group. "You said the meetings will be held in the club every evening. We are all for that. Now, brothers, let us go home ."

167

The group began to break up.

Meanwhile, Radwan had remained silent watching the proceedings from his secluded corner.

Every step they were taking increased his anxiety and alarm. He was now afraid that these events in the homeland would hinder his return, especially when he heard that the bombardments did not even spare the airport. This would definitely halt air travel and thus close the door to him.

When he went to bed that night, the world's worries and their distressing burdens went with him. He tossed from side to side, feeling as though he were sleeping on a bed of thorns.

Um Nabeel noticed his restlessness and asked, "What is the matter, husband?"

He did not answer. She tried again. "Are you in pain? What is the matter?"

"I can't sleep," he murmured.

His wife tried to soothe him with her kind words. "Perhaps it is because of what you saw on television. It is better for us not to watch or hear anything."

Radwan sat up. "Do you think one can do that, wife? How can our heart and our conscience allow it?"

"But worrying does not help," she answered "The best thing is to accept Nabeel's suggestion."

"Nabeel, may God be pleased with him! He has good ideas, but this will not help us."

"What do you mean, husband?"

"I mean that we must return, wife. And as soon as possible, before they close the borders and the airport."

"But the children will not allow that," she objected. "We promised to spend the holidays with them. We shouldn't disappoint them."

"Good luck to you, wife!" he answered sarcastically. "You are thinking of one thing while the world turns in a different direction! I am concerned about our destiny and our future, and whether we will be able to return home or not. And your mind is on the holidays!"

"My mind is on my children and grandchildren. I will stay with them until the holiday season is over. We don't get to visit Canada every day!"

"If you remain obstinate, you will be visiting Canada from now until the end of your life."

Um Nabeel fell silent and she sensed that her husband had reached the deepest levels of despair and worry. She shared his feelings but could not find any justification for an immediate return. She did not feel the same sudden fear that had possessed him and controlled his thinking.

Even if the Beirut airport were closed, she thought, there were other ways. She felt this but kept it to herself lest she should pour oil on fires already burning. Instead of arguing, she said calmly, "Let us sleep tonight. Tomorrow is another day. Trust in God, husband."

He did trust in God but the reins seemed to slip away from his hand occasionally and he went astray, falling into a bottomless abyss.

He turned off the light and tried to imitate his wife, wrapping himself up to calm the worry quivering in his heart, and drift into sleep.

168

His eyes never closed. Like grains of sand and splintered glass, his worry spread between his eyelids and his eyes, keeping him awake. Rain penetrated his body. In the dense darkness he saw the specter of a beautiful child with smiling lips, holding a daisy in his soft fingers and plucking its petals one by one, muttering, "She loves me, she loves me not... She loves me, she loves me not...."

He called the child to him. "I will teach you new words to say, do you hear me?"

The little one's lips trembled and he stepped back. Radwan's eyes followed him and saw the child turn into a horse trotting gently in the vast open spaces, then galloping through the forests of the Canadian north. Before the horse reached the horizon, he rose a few feet above the earth, then flew higher and higher until he became an eagle soaring in space, going farther and farther until he was only a tiny dot which soon disappeared in the sky.

169

They were not the cries of an eagle that Radwan heard with the sunrise the following day. He listened and counted: "Caw...caw...caw."

It was a black raven, "the raven of separation" as it was called in Jurat Al-Sindyan. The raven had come to caw at this early hour of the new day.

With his morning prayer, Radwan murmured, "May God spare us the evil of this day."

He tried to erase the idea from his mind as he remembered where he was.

No, you are not in Jurat Al-Sindyan, man. You are in Charlottetown. Birds here are not the same as there. Perhaps what you heard was not a raven anyway. It may have been another bird which has come to wake us up...

Besides, if the cry of a black raven is a bad omen pronouncing evil in your country, its story is different here, like many other things you have discovered. You have noticed how Maggie has an owl figurine in the middle of her entrance hall. She told you, "The owl brings good luck." Stores sell such owl figurines of all sizes and shapes made of colored glass or wax. Some have even been made into candles. Pictures of owls are on greeting cards. The owl for peep here brings happiness and good blessings. In Jurat Al-Sindyan it brings bad luck and destruction.

Who is right, now? And where do you stand? Why should the raven be different from the owl? They are both symbols of evil, but their story may be different here. Ask them when you get up, ask the young ones and they will tell you. Be optimistic, man. You are in a country which has discarded all superstitions and lives in day-to-day reality. Inherited traditions, old beliefs and tales of the past have nothing to do with its forward march. Man, you are in the land of the present.

170

With this hesitant thought, Radwan got up and went to the window. He raised the shade and saw a black bird moving about the trees in the garden, then perching on the bare branches of an apple tree next door. From there it cried, "Caw...caw."

It was indeed a raven, with all the usual characteristics. Its shape here was like its shape in Jurat Al-Sindyan. So were its color, its sound and its impudence! It was almost knocking at the door! The ravens of his homeland were satisfied with flying far above the houses so that their presence was limited to that ominous cawing.

He left the room and went down to the kitchen where the family usually gathered for breakfast.

The chairs were all empty. Salma was alone in the kitchen making coffee. Her back was to the door, so she did not see him enter.

"Good morning, my dear daughter."

She was startled at his voice and turned to him. "'Father? Oh, good morning! Did you sleep well?"

He shook his head. "It was a night of worries and night mares. The news from the homeland disturbed my nerves, dear. As if all that was not enough, there was this cawing bird which came before daybreak to utter its raucous call. May God spare us the evil of this day."

Salma did not seem to understand what he was saying and so he continued. "Have you heard its cawing, my daughter? Have you?

She smiled and tried to set his mind at ease. "Do you mean the raven? Oh, ravens abound on this Island. Flocks of them are everywhere, but they are not harmful."

"They are not harmful, we understand. But their cries are unbearable, my dear daughter."

His daughter-in-law agreed. "You are right. They don't have the beautiful melodies of goldfinches. But that is the gift of nature."

"That is not what I meant, daughter. Do you in Canada consider the cawing of the raven a bad omen?"

Salma shook her head. "No, never. People here don't stop to think of such things."

He surrendered. "People here have big minds. They are not concerned with little things."

Suddenly, as though he had just noticed the empty house, he asked, "Where are the young ones, dear? It seems they left early today."

Salma did not answer immediately, so he tried again. "It seems Nabeel is very busy these days!"

He kept silent for a few moments, waiting.

Salma then approached him, put her arm around his waist and said, "Nabeel and the young ones are at Mu'een's house. Uncle Saleem has passed away."

"Uncle Saleem? Impossible!"

He took a few steps backwards. "The Mukhtar is dead? What a good man we have lost!"

He then turned to his daughter-in-law. "Why didn't they tell me, daughter? They should have told me."

Salma answered, wiping her eyes, "I have stayed behind, waiting for you. After breakfast we will go together to Lamya's house.

171

What breakfast? Food at a time like this?

Radwan sat down to drink his coffee. The kitchen air was soon filled with cigarette smoke.

He did not have the courage to wake up Um Nabeel. So he waited for her.

Twice he almost reminded Salma of the dialogue he had just had with her moments before. He wanted to tell her that his intuition had told him some evil was going to happen and that the cawing of ravens was the omen. Canadian ravens' instincts, after all, were not different from those of Jurat Al-Sindyan.

He wanted to tell her this and more but his tongue would not obey. So he continued to ruminate on his thoughts and wait for Um Nabeel.

172

She was accustomed to his early rising. When she opened her eyes, she immediately looked for him. She went downstairs, grumbling at the slight whiffs of cold air coming from a draught.

He contemplated her as she came toward him, her eyes filled with joy.

"Good morning...."

He muttered a reply. Salma embraced her, inviting her to sit down for her coffee. Her husband's serious expression did not escape her. She saw the traces of last night's sleeplessness. She asked him as though speaking to herself, "It was a worrisome night, husband. Wasn't it?"

He looked at her intently but silently. He hesitated before answering. "It was a sweet night compared to the news of the day."

Fear jumped into her eyes. "Good news, God willing! Or is it bad news from the homeland?"

"News is bad from the homeland as well as from here," he answered calmly. "Uncle Saleem has passed away."

His words shocked her. The tragedy was portrayed on her face, in the veins of her hands and the shaking which overcame her body.

Her tears fell and a wailing sound escaped from her lips.

"It's so unfair! The death of good people is an injustice! What a grave loss! Uncle Saleem!"

She wiped her tears. "We must go at once and be with Lamya and Mu'een."

Salma patted her on the shoulder. "Take your time, you and my father-in-law. I will wait until you are both ready."

173

Death is silence and desolation. It is a mythical bird which spreads its wings over the community and drowns them in the abyss where they stand face to face with truth.

The community filled the funeral home. Mu'een sat silently. Next to him Lamya wiped her tears. Around them were the brothers and sisters, the relatives and the friends.

Um Nabeel reined in her feelings and did not allow herself to cry aloud, as she would have done in Jurat Al-Sindyan. The custom enumerated the fine qualities of the deceased, his good deeds and praiseworthy characteristics.

She approached her son-in-law, Mu'een, and embraced him. "It has been a great blow to us, my dear. The death of good people is an injustice!"

Then she turned to his brothers and repeated the traditional words. Radwan embraced his son-in-law and wept bitterly, shedding all the tears of his suppressed sorrow.

"What a grave loss Uncle Saleem's death is! What a grave loss!"

He glanced around at those present, then stood in front of them in the traditional way of Jurat Al-Sindyan, his right hand on his chest, his head slightly bowed, his words addressing all of them.

"May God compensate us with your safety."

Having performed the ritual, he sat down. But many questions knocked at the walls of his heart.

Why have they brought Al Mukhtar to this strange place when he has a large house and his son owns a home that is suitable to receive kings? Why?

He could not even ask his son Nabeel. He wanted to understand local customs. He spent the remaining hours of the day trying.

174

Saleem Waked had been getting ready to go to bed the previous evening when he felt a sharp pain in his chest. He realized immediately that it was another heart attack. He went directly to the telephone and called his son Mu'een. In a flash he was there with the doctor, but medicine was unable to save him this time. And so Councilman Saleem departed, ending a long and fruitful life.

Radwan sat calmly, questions simmering in his heart like water in a kettle.

What were the rituals of death in this country?

Why did silence reign instead of wailing and weeping?

And how about the songs for the dead? Where were the leaders of those laments who walk around the deceased, their loud wailing almost bringing the dead back to life? Where? Where were they?

He turned and saw Saad-Allah al-Hajj, the Mukhtar's friend, deep in silence, lost in a faraway world. He broke the silence between them. "Dear Saad-Allah, what are the customs in these circumstances?"

Saad-Allah returned from his distracted state, took a deep breath and replied, "The body of the deceased lies in state for two or more days until the burial time. This gives everyone a chance to pay their last respects to the deceased. The funeral home takes care of all matters relating to the funeral and the burial. This is done after the relatives are asked what kind of funeral rituals they want. There are ranks and levels in death as in life, Abu Nabeel."

Radwan could only say, "What a grave loss! May God have mercy on him!"

Deep inside he was grappling with another idea and comparing what he was seeing here with what used to happen at home. Here, people gathered to offer their condolences to the relatives of the deceased. Their words came out shyly, in whispers. No woman raised her voice, crying and wailing over the deceased and those who had gone before him. There were no laments in the courtyard of the house that whipped up the sorrow to a high intensity. There were no zajal folk poets coming from all the neighboring villages to recite elegies in alternating responses, giving the emotions free rein, making mourners slap their cheeks and cry their eyes out.

Radwan was sitting here in a foreign place, although it was dotted with the faces of loved ones, his children, his relatives and the people of his village.

Were they really people of his village? Why had they discarded the old traditions of sorrow?

He turned again to Saad-Allah and asked, "Are there no laments for the deceased, my friend?"

The man almost smiled at the naive question. "No, Abu Nabeel. These are customs we gave up long ago. As you see, if one feels the need to weep, he weeps — alone. Tell me, anyway, have the laments and the wailing ever brought a dead person back to life?"

Saad-Allah's words cleared the fog from Radwan's eyes. The man was telling the truth: singing never returned the dead to life, nor did the wailing of women or the wearing of black clothes. These were all traditions...mere traditions.

He answered his neighbor silently.

"That's true, my dear Saad-Allah, they are mere traditions. But when one of us feels that painful choking lump he needs to lean on an arm, throw himself on a breast, or even get lost in the memories of his past. The bite of pain no longer hurts, the wound heals, the distress calms down, and the cold retreats to be replaced by a comfortable warmth which penetrates his being and connects him to his surroundings.

"I tell you, my dear Saad-Allah, each of us dies alone as he was born alone. But death loses its terror when we turn around and find comforting familiar faces. Or when we listen, and kind loving voices come to our ears, rocking us into peaceful sleep in the arms of the earth like a baby sleeps in the lap of his mother.

"I tell you, my dear Saad-Allah, these are not tangible things. It may be difficult for you and me to explain and understand them. But they are important to people who practice them."

He then raised his voice, answering the question still suspended in the air: "No, of course not, my dear Saad-Allah. Laments and wailing never resurrected the dead."

175

Man here dies twice: first when he stops breathing and his heart rests. The second time is when they accompany him to his last abode.

His last abode!

"Will your last abode be here, Mukhtar?"

Radwan asked, but Al Mukhtar did not answer. Nor did he move to explain to Radwan difficult matters which he did not understand. Instead, the priest came forth in a white robe and murmured some prayers in the language of the people of Canada.

Al Mukhtar was inside a tightly sealed box.

The priest ended his prayer and dismissed the people.

Radwan understood all that from the movement of those who had come to pay their last respects.

Close family left first and waited in a nearby hall, followed by all the others attending the funeral. They all shook hands and offered their sympathies.

The casket was taken care of by the funeral home's employees.

176

When the procession moved on to bury Al Mukhtar in his final resting place, only a few people went: his sons, his older grandchildren and some relatives. Radwan insisted on going too, but Mu'een objected.

"It is better that you return home with my mother-in-law. We don't want you to wear yourself out."

Radwan rejected this with determination. "This is my duty to God, my son. God will grant me strength. What is the world without this kind of sharing and care, my dear Mu'een?"

He crossed the short distance between the church and the cemetery. Radwan fell deep into thought, meditating on man's destiny, from the moment he opened his eyes until he closed them and departed. He then moved on to think of Al Mukhtar and he wondered if Saleem had not been born in this country, would he have wanted to be buried here?

Man, you are always thinking of difficulties. When a person dies, he no longer feels anything, whether he is buried in alien soil or under the snow at the North Pole, whether he is cremated or buried at sea. He feels no difference. He is finished. His soul has departed. Earth returns to earth, and the body blends into the elements that nourished it during its brief existence on earth.

177

Earth opened her arms and received the coffin through her wide door. Then the door was closed. The mourners returned through heavy rain mixed with snow. The wind blew fiercely.

178

How cold the last resting place was in this country!

How lonely, desolate and cold was death in a strange land!

They left Al Mukhtar silently and reverently. The procession returned to the city of the living, then everyone went about his own business.

This was all the dead were given by the living: a few hours that passed slowly and heavily. Radwan felt that the earth was shaking under his feet, as if it were a carpet and he was being tossed off. For a few moments, he flew beyond time and space, then returned to his place in a comfortable chair at the home of his son-in-law. He was unable to rein in his subconscious and prevent it from bringing out all the images stacked in his memory. He continued this comparison of past and present, which always seemed to lead him to one conclusion.

He rejected the customs he had not grown up with. He felt that his mind did not obey nor did his emotions submit. The matter was not as simple as drinking a cup of coffee. It was the relationship of man to the living and the dead and to everything that surrounded him.

179

Radwan sat in a quiet place after the tiring day. Sleep crept to his eyelids and closed them, sending him away as a light transparent body would float on a cloud the color of dawn.

He wondered secretly: where would the cloud take him? Did it follow a definite line of flight like the jumbo jet which carried him to this country?

Was he embarking on a long, long trip? Where would it take him?

He heard a voice rising in the tranquillity, calling to him to come closer.

He looked around for the source of the voice but saw nobody. He intuitively understood that Al Mukhtar was calling him. What could he want?

"Come closer, my dear Abu Nabeel," he said. "Come closer so that I may whisper in your ear this small secret. I am telling you that the journey is not frightening. The end has been easy, with no disease or pain. As quick as a wink. Have you understood me, Abu Nabeel? Like when you blow out a candle. Here I am now, comfortable...comfortable."

Radwan could not help saying, "But you did not say good-bye to anyone. You surprised us. You left us with two burning agonies."

"What do you mean, Abu Nabeel?"

"It is unfair to lose you now, my brother. Life still suits you well. You left us suddenly, our grief is great and—"

Al Mukhtar did not let him continue. "I know what you are thinking... Thank God, I have lived my life and my children have become adults. I have done my duty to them and to society. I was ready to go."

"But this does not prevent our great grief. Separation is difficult. Besides, if death had taken place in the homeland, everything would have been different. Do you understand me, Mukhtar? Everything would have been different."

"These are secondary matters, Abu Nabeel. The important thing is the essence. There is always a place for sorrow. Don't let it overcome you. Try to explain this to the people of the mahjar, the land of emigration."

180

Radwan jumped as if he had been stung. He raised his hand and rubbed his eyes. Gradually, he returned to his surroundings.

He had not been asleep more than a moment. How could all this conversation have taken place? And with Al Mukhtar?

He knew from stories that before the soul finally left the earth, it continued to wander about in bewilderment for some time. Its time of wandering lengthened if the end was sudden as in cases of murder or massive heart attacks. Did Al Mukhtar's soul visit him to say farewell? Why did it choose him? What did he say?

He tried to remember every word and began to watch the film in reverse. He became convinced that Al Mukhtar had chosen him for a message to erase the sorrow deep in his heart and the worry embedded in his soul.

Yet he did not want to stay and die here, however easy the death trip was. He wanted everybody to say good-bye to him with songs, in laments, with the traditional tunes that helped one approach the places of joy.

He wanted to see around him all those he loved and those who loved him in that warm corner of the earth. He wanted the wailing women to surround him and the female mourner to raise her voice, enumerate his good deeds, to seek everyone's abundant tears, and remember all the dead who preceded, inviting them to accompany him on the paths of this new trip.

Why are you thinking of death when you are in the best of health, man? his inner voice asked.

Indeed, my health is excellent. But a human being is frail. A mere puff sends him flying away. Look at Al Mukhtar, for example.

The voice continued.

You are a pessimist, man. You only see the dark side of things and blind yourself to all the shining moons and bright faces.

He shouted angrily, I see the truth! I am not blind! I see both worlds, everything, here and there!

He heard roaring laughter within. You are strange! Two days ago you were laughing and joking with your cousin Shaheen. Do you remember the story Shaheen told you about the goldfinch?

The question brought back his sense of humor.

Shaheen? Is Shaheen's story credible? He carried a goldfinch from the other side of the world, from the orchards of Hasbaya, and smuggled it into Canada to put it in a cage.

The inner voice interrupted politely, And then, what happened?

What happened was that the goldfinch lived a few months, then died. Shaheen swore he would bury it in the soil of Hasbaya. Because he could not travel to the homeland, the poor bird is still enshrined in the refrigerator... Is this a credible thing, Shaheen's act, I mean?

The voice took revenge on him and continued the dialogue. Then you agree with me. As far as the bird is concerned, there is no difference between being frozen for ten years or being buried in a Canadian or Hasbani orchard!

Radwan felt he was slipping into the trap set up for him. He shouted, Is the goldfinch a human being? I am speaking of human beings, I am speaking about a man of position like Al Mukhtar. Is such a burial proper for Al Mukhtar? Tell me the truth, tell me...

The voice did not say a word. It left him perplexed and flew away. He could almost hear the flapping of its wings. He even imagined that he heard the echo of laughter which did not resemble that of a human.

He sat up and opened his eyes. He took a cigarette from his pocket, lit it and let his thoughts float amidst the clouds of smoke.

181

Dawn stealthily penetrated the layers of dense clouds and poured its light on the Island. Then it waited.

No one rushed to greet it. Doors remained closed, windows wore layers of drapes, and not a single curtain winked a sign of welcome.

Radwan was in a room lined with drapes, insulated and dark—an atom of life in a self-enclosed cocoon.

How long would he be able to tolerate the situation?

He asked himself these questions as soon as he opened his eyes in the morning, and determined that he would make his decision known before sunset that day. He would not remain on the Island one more day. He would pack up his clothes and return. Yes, he would return, come what may. Let Heaven fall down to Earth. But no, Heaven would not fall down to Earth. All that might happen would be that his children would oppose his idea. He would obstinately insist. They might well prevent Um Nabeel from accompanying him. She was free, he thought, she was free to choose her children and grandchildren, and stay with them after she had been his companion for half a century.

"Um Nabeel, fifty years have passed since our first meeting. My steps have accompanied yours inseparably on our common path. Now you say you prefer to stay here?"

She would raise her voice and maybe shout at him for the first time: "But you are embarking on a dangerous venture, husband. It is sheer madness to travel to the homeland now!"

"Madness or no madness — this is what I have decided!"

Nabeel would intervene. "The question is not one of standing by your words or carrying out your decisions, Father. There is a greater danger than any of us can deal with. People are fleeing Lebanon and you are going back. Why?"

Nawal would support his brother: "As long as we are all here, Father, all your children, your own flesh and blood, as well as your grandchildren and Um Nabeel, your love and life's companion. . .to whom exactly are you returning?"

He would look into Nawal's face and say nothing.

Hassan would challenge him. "Nawal has asked you an important question. Why don't you answer? Who is waiting for you there?"

He would remain silent.

He would prefer silence to hurting them with his answer. He'd say, "There is one waiting for me. My beloved, my village, is eagerly waiting for me. She is leaning on Mount Hermon, opening her arms with longing to enfold me in her warm lap. . .there, where I planted seventy years of my life."

Lamya would ask, "Does she love you more than we do? I don't think so."

Jameel would agree with her, "Lamya is speaking for everyone. All your loved ones are around you here, your children, your grandchildren.... You have come here to spend a few months — a few months, not days."

They would besiege him on all sides, pointing their good-hearted weapons at him: love shining in their eyes and kindness coming from their lips. They would besiege him, come closer to him, clasp their hands around him. He would become their captive. He would look for an escape but find none.

When he was little, he used to play this game with his friends. They would hold hands and turn in a circle while one of them was a prisoner inside. The prisoner would look for a way out. He would try to break through by using all the ruses he had until he succeeded and escaped...

Now he did not see any opening. The circle of arms around him was getting tighter as though the five beings of his own flesh and blood were again joining forces and becoming one.

His eyes would seek Um Nabeel, hoping she would change her mind and oppose them. But his life's companion would remain silent.

182

He left her to her silence and her morning sleep, and stole out of the room to escape the disturbing thoughts attacking him with the dawn of a new day.

And as he had seen them in his dream, he saw them sitting in a circle around the kitchen table, talking in whispers.

He sensed that he was the topic of conversation and was dismayed. He was afraid that the dialogue of his dream would become a real conversation.

He hastened to find out. "What is the news of the homeland? Good news I hope."

Their eyes met momentarily before Nabeel replied, "The news is terrible. The situation is going from bad to worse."

"Is that what the radio says?"

"The radio, television and newspapers," Hassan answered. "All the media speak of nothing but Lebanon."

Radwan nodded his head sadly. "Did the war have to happen before they would take an interest in us?"

"This is exactly what happened," Nawal replied. "If it were not for the war, we wouldn't have heard any news of the homeland. It is unfortunate that our age is nourished on sensational stories."

"What do you think, Nawal?" Radwan asked her. "Is the war going to last?"

She answered simply, "We know when the war starts, Father, but we don't know when it ends. Only God knows that."

He tossed out a question, testing them. "So, what is to be done?"

Nabeel said boldly, "At the family level, we thank God that you are both here. This at least relieves us from anxiety. At the national level, our Lebanese brothers and sisters are enthusiastic about the meetings and we hope our efforts will be fruitful."

"For my part, I prefer to return to Jurat Al-Sindyan before the situation gets worse."

Radwan's reply shocked them.

"This is impossible!" Lamya cried. "We will not allow you and Mother to return to the homeland at the present time. People are escaping from Lebanon in little boats, on board cargo ships...."

"People are free, my daughter. Everyone does what suits him. My feeling is that I should return."

"Father, let us speak frankly," Hassan interjected. "Your return will not benefit the homeland. It may be the biggest danger ever to your lives."

Radwan said with certainty, "No one dies before his appointed time, before the coming of his hour."

His answer silenced them, touching their unsaid longing, as eager as his own, to return to the homeland.

When he approached the boundaries of this open wound, he felt he had won a victory over them, at least for the moment. He had put his finger on their point of weakness and defeat — the harshness of their alienation.

He left them, sitting around the table, as he went toward the window. A tableau of snow and ice surrounded the house.

A snowstorm had begun on the Island two days before, fed by the air currents from the North Pole. His eyes saw nothing but white space.

There was white on the ground, on the trees, in the air — falling from a sky so low it almost knelt to the ground.

On a day like this, he yearned for the fireplace in Jurat Al-Sindyan. He would feed it with oak logs and old-time stories, and then enjoy the warmth that reached deep inside him. He longed to hear the voices of the neighbors, meeting on the roofs shoveling snow, cooperating across the alleys and front yards, as their voices filled the air with friendly greetings.

This snow moved his yearning for warmth just as his alienation from this land moved his longing for the roots he had left there in the depths of the earth.

183

To those depths he sought to return. They pulled him from the top of his head to the bottoms of his feet. He followed them, enchanted as though a magnet were moving him and he had no power or will of his own.

He heard an inner voice calling. What is happening is by your own willful design, man. You turn a deaf ear to all the voices and run away. All the voices tell you it's madness, you are embarking on an act of madness. A rational man would listen to his children. They know, better than you do, what is happending there. They are doing the impossible to warm your winter days.

They did not say a word to disturb you, they did not cast a look to embarrass you. They were all love and kindness, they and their spouses, and the grandchildren. Yet you run away from this bliss which enfolded you like a mother's lap. You said to yourself that you were full of yearning, that your land was burning. . .your sweetheart was writhing under the cracking of whips. What are you able to do when the war is spreading over the entire homeland? In the past, you could intervene between fighters in Jurat Al-Sindyan. But there is a great difference between the past and the present days, between Jurat Al-Sindyan's fights that used clubs and stones and today's war that shakes the corners of the homeland, its news spreading over the globe.

You are now at the other edge of the sea, on this vast and great continent. The news followed you to your bed and was indeed the most important subject they spoke about. You can behave like a reasonable man, stay with the young ones, and follow the news in colored pictures. You should think of the dire consequences, man. You should think of the young ones and the mother of the young ones.... You should abandon your own desires, just a little, for the sake of those you love....

184

Radwan withdrew from the window and went immediately to the bedroom. Um Nabeel's bed was empty. He noticed she was in the bathroom.

He did not call her as he usually did, but went to his suitcase and began packing.

His wife surprised him before he had finished.

"I see you are perplexed, husband. What is the matter?"

He looked at her like a child caught red-handed.

"Nothing is the matter, wife. You woke up late today."

"True, I'm late. It was dark and quiet, and I thought morning had not yet dawned."

He answered mockingly, "It has dawned and the sun is already in the middle of the sky."

She almost believed him, had she not noticed his cunning smile. She raised the shade and the whiteness struck her eyes.

"It has been snowing, and we didn't even know it."

"You were sleeping peacefully, Um Nabeel."

She asked, "And yet, you got up early!"

She then noticed the open suitcase.

"And what is this, husband? Traveling again? We have just arrived!"

"We have just been traveling and now we are preparing for another trip. I am going back home."

"This is sheer madness! Unbelievable! What will people say of us? They will blame the young ones. Have pity on your children, husband!"

"I have made up my mind." His tone did not change. "Everyone is free to decide what he wants."

When his wife did not move, he continued, "And you, my wife, you are free to stay with the children for a month or two or three... I will go first and you can follow."

Um Nabeel was silent. Words froze in her throat. She felt she was standing in front of a stranger. He was extremely different. She wondered whether the trip had affected him, causing him to make important decisions without consulting anyone, ignoring the pleas of those who cared for him.

She thought again and tried to deal with the perplexing question before her: should she accompany him or stay with her children?

Why did he make her face such a difficult choice? She had not seen her children for long enough. She was looking forward to the holiday season. She wanted to know more about the lives of each one of them so that when the day came to leave, she could go with a good provision of memories and peace of mind.

Now he had put her in an impossible situation and she did not know how to answer. She decided to leave it up to the young ones.

"Nabeel will decide for me. I am a guest of my children and I leave the decision up to them."

He did not say a word. He continued to pack his belongings in an orderly manner. When the suitcase was full, he locked it and put the key in his pocket.

185

Um Nabeel left him and went downstairs. She suddenly felt that the burden was too big for her and she needed the help of the young ones.

They received her cheerfully, but their cheerfulness disappeared when they saw her eyes.

She summed up the situation simply: "Your father has packed up."

Hassan leapt up from his chair. "As far as I'm concerned, I will never speak to him again! It is finished! A partnership has been broken!"

"Take it easy, Hassan," Nabeel said, putting his hand on his brother's shoulder to calm him. "We have tried to convince him and failed. Now we have to help him leave without breaking his heart."

Hassan looked at him in anger. "Sometimes I don't understand you, Nabeel. Will you carry the responsibility for his safety?"

Nabeel smiled sadly. "You heard him, Hassan, we have all heard him. He is fully resigned to his fate. He is with us in body, but his soul is in Jurat Al-Sindyan."

Hassan did not like these words and could not conceal his anger. He went out, slamming the door behind him, leaving the others in dismay.

Nabeel took his mother's hand. "Don't worry, Mother. My father does what gives him inner peace. We will let him leave but we won't let you go. He is stronger than you, he can move about more easily. As for you, you will stay here with us."

She murmured through her tears, "All these years, we have never been apart. On all paths of life, we have always been together. What has happened now to change this?"

Lamya and Nawal went over to her and put their arms around her, while Jameel bent to kiss her forehead.

"You will stay with us until the danger is gone. Our father can manage alone."

"What if the war continues for a long time?" she implored.

"We will not tie you up with ropes," Nabeel reassured her. "Whenever you want to leave, we will arrange everything for you, even accompany you on the trip."

She was thinking beyond that. She was thinking of her husband. What if something should happen to him, would she ever forgive herself for staying behind with her children?

She turned to Nabeel. "Suppose, my son, that something bad did happen—God forbid—what would we do?"

Nabeel tightened his arm around her waist. "None of us would then be able to stop the evil. We must resign ourselves to God's will."

186

That Supreme Will was leading them towards the airport, as soon as the snowstorm cleared and the first airplane could leave.

The sky had dumped the temperament of the North Pole on the airport grounds, on people's heads, and on the trees. The family was huddled in a warm corner in the terminal, waiting for the gate to open to the plane.

They were quiet—not a word or sign was exchanged.

Only the young ones had come to see him off. They had not told relatives and friends. They had brought the grandchildren to say good-bye to their grandfather.

Their grandfather was going through the trial of his life. He kissed them all. He kissed them several times and wept bitterly. His eyes became red, his lips quivered and he felt Canada's cold settle between his shoulder blades.

His children looked on, pondering this unique experience. They were unable to perceive the significance of what was happening. They felt that an invisible hand had risen beyond their power, had numbed them and made them stand like statues to witness and record the rhythm of time.

That invisible hand stretched out to take away the man who had come to visit like an image in a dream.

187

From the airplane window, his hand waved a white handkerchief that had been softened by tears.

From the airplane window...

Their eyes remained fixed on that point until the plane moved, then took off and became just a hazy point in space.

Epilogue

1

News Bulletin

They found him at a road intersection leading to all the southern villages.

His body was stretched out like a cross.

The ambulance of the Hasbaya municipality carried him to the government hospital at Marji'yoon.

The doctor who examined him wrote in his report: "Radwan Abu Yusef (70 years), from the village of Jurat Al-Sindyan belonging to the district of Hasbaya, was carried to the hospital and found dead on arrival. Upon medical examination, it was found that his body was covered with bruises, wounds and fractures. They were especially prevalent in the chest area where X-rays showed that all his ribs were broken. In addition, the X-rays revealed fractures of the skull and the vertebral column, causing his death ten hours prior to the examination."

January 20, 1976

2

The report of the Mukhtar of Jurat Al-Sindyan said the following:

Citizen Radwan Abu Yusef (70 years) was kidnapped from his home at nine o'clock on the evening of January 18, 1976. All efforts to find him or to identify the kidnappers failed. The victim was at his home that night. With him was a group of neighbors and friends. Three armed men wearing disguises knocked at the door and asked him to accompany them. They asked him to identify an unknown suspect who, they claimed, was found near the village. Radwan enthusiastically went out to offer help. A few steps beyond the threshold, the three men pointed their weapons at him and at anyone who made a sound. They took him in a landrover to an unknown place. About six o'clock in the morning of January 20, 1976, and thirty-three hours after the kidnapping, a certain driver found the body of the victim lying on the side of the road. He hastened to the Hasbaya police station and informed the authorities. An ambulance carried the body to the government hospital at Marji'yoon where the district medical officer, Dr. F.N., examined it.

Note: This is the third incident of its kind in the district in one month. All victims were innocent citizens.

> S.F.
> Mukhtar of Jurat Al-Sindyan

3

Local newspaper report
Jurat Al-Sindyan, January 25, 1976

The funeral of Radwan Abu Yusef took place today. The village had never witnessed such a well-attended event as this one, in either its ancient or recent history.

Beginning at dawn, the people of the neighboring villages began arriving in groups, from the north and the south, from the east and the west. They belonged to all religious sects and political parties.

Young men and women wept, as did the old people and the children.

The sky, too, shed abundant tears. The church bell tolled, accompanied by the voices of mourners, women in black clothing with white shawls over their heads, and women dressed completely in black.

The bell tolled to the wailing of men who had formed several groups, competing with each other in praising the departed.

Leading the mourners were Muslim sheykhs, Christian priests and the notables of the village.

The wife of the deceased and two of his sons, Nabeel and Hassan, had arrived from Canada as soon as they heard of the tragic event.

4

A Strange Phenomenon

On the eve of Radwan Abu Yusef's burial, Jurat Al-Sindyan spoke about a strange phenomenon which people related on the authority of the midwife Um Naaman, one of the ablest and most experienced women in matters of birth and death.

Um Naaman said that Radwan's forehead perspired the entire time he was lying in state at the church, and that his face appeared sometimes to be cheerful, with a light smile hovering between his lips and his eyes. When she informed the two sons of this, they did not comment.

5

A Dialogue Towards the End of Night

Nabeel: What do you think of Um Naaman's words, Hassan?

Hassan: I saw what Um Naaman saw, but I didn't dare say anything lest people begin to gossip.

Nabeel: You mean the sweat or the smile?

Hassan: I mean both. Medical doctors may find an acceptable explanation for the sweat, but how can we explain the smile?

Nabeel: Come on, Hassan! Don't you have an explanation?

Hassan: I may have one, but I won't say it.

Nabeel: Then I will say it for you. I tell you that the shadow of a smile is our father's secret message to us and to all his friends. He wanted to thank them, to say they had not disappointed him but as he had hoped and expected, they surrounded him with all their love. They came from all directions, from all religions, of all ages, to his funeral. Perhaps the circumstances of war did not permit a great reception to welcome the man arriving from America. So they all showed up today to tell him that he was still among them, that his crossing of the continents and the seven seas and his flight against time had not been in vain. He is well-remembered. His name is recorded in their hearts and in their eyes. Today, they wrote him a love letter with their tears. The unknown kidnappers tortured his body but his soul soars beyond their reach. It rises above hatred and revenge, it rises high with forgiveness and love. If our father could speak, Hassan, he would have said what the Lord said two thousand years ago: "Father, forgive them for they know not what they do."